Audrey Goes to Town

The Audrey Club!

If you love reading *Audrey* stories, join Audrey's fan club to read more!

- You will receive a postcard from Audrey!
- FREE updates on Audrey via *The Outback Post*.
- Enter Audrey competitions.
- FREE Audrey giveaways.
- The chance to have the author, Christine Harris, visit your school.

To join send your mailing address inside an envelope to:
Little Hare Books, 8/21 Mary Street,
Surry Hills, NSW, 2010
or visit www.audreyoftheoutback.com.au

*You will need to get Mum or Dad or your guardian to send a permission note in your email or envelope!

I want a dad who rides a camel
to work. —Jack, age 8

Audrey
goes to
Town

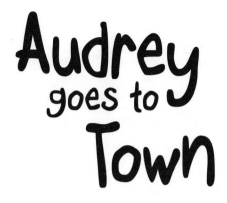

Christine Harris

Illustrations by Ann James

LITTLE ⟶ HARE
www.littleharebooks.com

For Ben, who shines as brightly as Audrey—CH

For Tash and Ash—who like to look and wonder—AJ

Little Hare Books
8/21 Mary Street, Surry Hills
NSW 2010 AUSTRALIA

www.littleharebooks.com

Text copyright © Christine Harris 2008
Illustrations copyright © Ann James 2008
Cover illustration copyright © Ann James 2008

First published in 2008

National Library of Australia
Cataloguing-in-Publication entry
Harris, Christine, 1955- .
Audrey goes to town / Christine Harris ; illustrator, Ann James.

978 1 921272 67 7 (pbk.)
For primary school age.

James, Ann.

A823.3

Cover design by Natalie Winter
Set in 13/18pt Stone Informal by Clinton Ellicott
Printed in China by WKT Company Limited

5 4 3 2 1

About the Author

Christine Harris has lived in different parts of South Australia, some of them isolated country areas.

The directions to one of her houses went like this: 'the first fridge on the right, fifteen kilometres after the last pub'. Kangaroos jumped past her kitchen window, and she once found a snake skin in the shed.

She spent much of her childhood in the wild places of her imagination, as a princess in a castle, a pirate on the wild seas, an archaeologist. Even her best friend, Jennifer Hobbar, was imaginary. But Christine only realised this when she tried to visit Jennifer's house and had no idea where it was.

Christine believes the Outback draws you back to visit, again and again. She also believes that, with a vivid imagination, you can travel anywhere.

www.christineharris.com

Audrey could hardly wait to get to Beltana.

One

Audrey Barlow bounced as the wheels of the wooden cart hit a pothole. Although the floor was padded with blankets and what was left in the food bags, each bump jarred Audrey and her brothers.

Douglas fell sideways, giggling. He was only three, so he giggled at nearly everything.

'Sesiting, isn't it?' said Audrey.

'*Ex*citing.' Price tried to sit straight and tall, as though he didn't care about the roughness of the bush track or the town

1

they would reach that afternoon. But his eyes shone.

Eucalyptus trees grew on the wide plain. Although the sand was not as red as back home, the grey saltbush was familiar. And there were tufts of green grass. Maybe it rained more in the south. A grey rabbit scurried across the track, its tail and ears flashing white.

Audrey looked up at her parents on the high front seat of the cart. Mum had been unusually quiet for most of the trip. Her face was pale. Audrey wondered if Mum's leg was hurting. Years earlier, a tank stand had crushed it, so she walked with a limp.

Dad turned his head to peer at Audrey from beneath the brim of his battered hat. His bushy beard fluttered in the wind. 'Not far now, Two-Bob.'

She grinned. Dad always used her nick-name. A swaggie called Bloke had given Audrey that name when she'd said, 'You're as crazy as a two-bob watch.'

Swaggies usually avoided towns. But Audrey could hardly wait to get to Beltana. From her home in the bush, it was three days' walk to the nearest house. And a lot more than that to a town.

'Dad, are the houses in Beltana really right next to each other, in rows?' asked Audrey.

'Sure as eggs.'

'There won't be so many flies because there's more people to share them.' Back home, flies stuck to their backs like dark coats. Especially on north wind days.

Suddenly Mum grabbed Dad's arm. 'Stop!'

Two

Mum half-dropped, half-jumped to the ground without waiting for Dad's help.

Audrey exchanged a surprised look with Price.

Their mum bent over, her arms cradling her stomach, and began retching into the saltbushes.

Douglas slipped his hand into Audrey's and squeezed. Silence settled on the family. The only sound was Mum going for the big spit, and the wind hissing dust.

Dad stood, holding the camels steady. His

rough hands were as battered as his hat. Dirt stained his fingernails. Dad narrowed his eyes and stared at the Flinders Ranges on the horizon. Audrey guessed he was trying not to make Mum feel awkward about being sick.

He slipped the reins into his left hand and, with his right, patted his top pocket. Although he had given up tobacco, he still liked to chew on the empty clay pipe. He fumbled as he took it from his pocket and the pipe fell to the ground.

Snort lifted one of his large flat feet and crushed it.

Dad glared at his camel, then down at the crumbs of his favourite pipe.

'Snort's in twubble,' said Douglas.

'Snort's *always* in trouble.' Audrey wriggled her fingers. They were starting to tingle from her little brother's tight grip.

Dad must have been very worried if he could watch his pipe get smashed and not say naughty words.

Mrs Barlow reached into her pocket for a handkerchief. She turned to face the family. Her skin was shiny with perspiration. She moved her mouth into the shape of a smile, but it didn't look real.

'Are you all right?' asked Audrey.

Mrs Barlow nodded. 'I'm not a good traveller.'

Dad gave Mum a funny look like he wanted to say something but couldn't. He offered Mum his hand. She took it and climbed back onto the front seat of the cart.

As they began moving again, Mum's back was straight and she didn't take her eyes off the track ahead. But she gripped the seat with both hands as though she might slide off. Audrey had a strange feeling, as though someone had whispered something important and she'd missed what was said.

Three

A glint of light to the left of the track caught Audrey's attention. She blinked hard. It was the kind of warm, clear afternoon when mirages shimmered in the distance. But this glint was real.

'I can see the railway line!' she shouted. 'I wish a train would come past so we could hear the driver blow the whistle.'

'There's the station,' said Price. The tremble in his voice gave away a hidden thrill at seeing the first building.

'Where?'

Price pointed.

At first, all Audrey saw were trees. Then she spotted an iron roof. She didn't mind that Price had been first to notice the station. She'd seen the railway line before anyone else.

'I want to see the fing too.' Douglas tugged at Audrey's sleeve.

She wasn't sure that her little brother knew what that *thing* was. Douglas sometimes became excited without understanding why.

As they drew closer, the station building seemed to grow larger. The platform was hidden on the other side of the building. Three Aboriginal men sat together with their backs against the wall. One of the men nodded a greeting. Audrey and Douglas waved.

The track widened. Two carts could have passed each other, side-by-side.

A flapping cloud of feathers and noise rose from a tree. The screeching pink-and-white cockatoos made Audrey jump. Her mother laughed. Audrey was glad that Mum was feeling better. Their trip was almost over. Perhaps, when the cart stopped rocking, so would her mum's stomach.

To the right of the track, mounds and headstones showed a graveyard. Audrey pictured the wooden crosses at home that marked the resting place of her two sisters, Pearl and Esther. Here in town, people were buried with many of their friends. Even when they died, they were not alone.

Just past the graveyard, a large dam reflected the blue of the sky.

'Strike a light,' shouted Audrey. 'Look at all that water.'

'That's for the steam trains,' said Dad.

'Town's an amazing place. They even water their trains!'

Four

'What's that, Pwice?' shouted Douglas, pointing to a building on the edge of town.

'It's the telegraph station. You can send messages and letters from there.'

'Whenever you want?' said Audrey.

'I guess so.'

At home the Barlow family used to wait for Mr Akbar to turn up on his camel with their mail. Sometimes it was months between visits. Now the mail was supposed to come in a truck. So far, that hadn't happened. Maybe the new mailman was still trying to find their house.

Audrey ran her tongue over the grit on her front teeth. She couldn't do anything about the dust on her skin. Her fair hair was tied into plaits, but a few loose strands always escaped. Her mother sometimes said she looked like something the cat dragged in. Which wasn't really true. They didn't have a cat.

After the telegraph station, there were houses along proper town roads. Most of the ramshackle buildings sat on bare dirt. Audrey had imagined gardens so green they would be too vivid to look at without blinking. There were trees, but no grass. Not even saltbush.

'Leaping lizards!' Audrey called out, 'Those houses have glass in their windows.'

'So will ours, one day, Two-Bob,' said Dad. 'You wait and see.'

They rattled past a hotel. It had a long verandah decorated with green plants in tubs. Laughter billowed out of the open windows. After the hotel there were more houses and then a tiny school. The schoolyard was silent.

'It's holiday time,' Dad explained.

Then Audrey smelled something familiar. Fresh bread! Dad had told her Beltana had a real bakery. Not just an outside oven made from crushed ants' nests, as they had at home.

On the road were other carts, riders on horses, an Afghan on a camel, and people walking. Audrey wanted to look in every direction at once. Her neck was becoming sore from turning her head left, right, then left again.

A plump Aboriginal woman with a scarf wrapped around her hair smiled as their cart went by. Audrey waved.

Then she heard loud rumbling and twisted around for a better look. A dust-covered black car had turned onto the road behind them. Douglas threw himself, headfirst, onto Audrey's lap. His elbow hit her shin. His words were buried in the folds of her blue smock dress.

The noisy car quickly caught up to the cart, its tyres whipping up dust. More dust than a camel would make, or a horse. More than *two* horses. Audrey glimpsed the driver's long, dark sleeves and hat. Then the car passed and they were swallowed up in a cloud of dust. The camels pulling the Barlows' cart snorted and sped up.

'Stay close,' Audrey reminded her friend Stumpy. If he ran off by himself, she might not be able to find him. Price rolled his eyes.

Douglas lifted his head. 'It's gwowling. It's got a tummy ache.'

'It's not growling, Dougie,' said Price. 'The car has a motor to make it go.'

Audrey felt a bubble of excitement. Anything could happen in town.

The front door opened and a tall, old lady marched out.

Five

A little further along, a herd of goats strayed onto the road. They bleated and refused to obey the bald man who was trying to guide them. The goats were like naughty children, each wanting to go their own way.

Douglas sat up and stuck his thumb in his mouth. Gently, Audrey tugged at his hand. His thumb popped out. The second she let go, it went back in as though it was on a length of elastic.

On the last road in town, Dad pulled on

the reins and the camels came to a grumpy stop. The cart wheels crunched on gravel.

'Here we are,' said Dad.

The big house stood alone, facing the plains. Large windows at the front of the house looked like eyes, except they were shut. Dark-green ivy covered the front wall. If it grew any more, it would block the doorway.

'Dad, is there another door at the back?' asked Audrey.

He nodded.

'Mrs Pat ... Patingsin must be rich if she's got two doors.'

Dad leapt down onto the dusty road. 'The lady's name is Paterson, Two-Bob. Better get it right.'

'Pancakes,' said Douglas.

'Are you hungry, Dougie?' Audrey smiled at her little brother.

Price jumped to the ground by himself. Dad helped Mum down, then Douglas and last of all, Audrey.

She felt her stomach flutter as she looked at the big house.

Stumpy stood back, restless and snorting.

The front door opened and a tall, old lady marched out. She was dressed in black, from her high-buttoned collar down to her ankles. She looked like a burnt stick.

As the lady opened her gate, Dad put one hand to the brim of his hat and tilted it. He didn't shake hands with girls and ladies. Only men. Dad had a strong grip. Maybe he was worried he'd squash girls' hands. 'Afternoon, Mrs Paterson.'

Mrs Paterson's grey hair was pulled back into a tight bun. A good share of wrinkles creased her face. Her nose was sharp enough to open a can of peaches and her mouth drooped at the corners.

Audrey's mum stepped forward and smiled. 'Thank you for asking us to stay, Mrs Paterson.'

'I have a large house and one tries to be charitable.'

Mum's smile disappeared.

Mrs Paterson's voice made Audrey think of water dripping into the dark well at home.

Dad introduced them all.

There was something about the way the old lady eyed them up and down that reminded Audrey of her dad inspecting stock.

'You must be tired and hungry,' said Mrs Paterson. 'Come inside. Do be careful to close the gate properly. Otherwise the goats will eat everything.'

'Pancakes,' demanded Douglas.

'I *beg* your pardon?' Mrs Paterson's mouth tightened like a shrivelled quandong.

Suddenly, a month in town seemed a long time.

Six

The Barlow family sat around Mrs Paterson's kitchen table.

Although the kitchen was large, it was so neat that Audrey wondered how often the old lady sat there. There were cupboards with doors, not just stacked wooden crates like home. And the glass window over the sink was covered by net curtains. They had gone yellow in places from the sun and Audrey could see where they had been mended. But they were proper curtains.

There was a soft shiny covering on the floor, with a blue flower pattern.

'That's linoleum, dear,' said Mum, with a wistful look.

The floor at home was rammed mud. In summer, Audrey's family sprinkled it with water so it didn't crack in the heat.

Audrey ran her fingers down the fat leg of the solid kitchen table. The wood was smooth, cool and straight. Everything Dad made was as crooked as a dog's hind leg. But no one minded. A navy-and-red checked cloth covered Mrs Paterson's table. Audrey put her palm against the cloth. It felt stiff.

Then the rich aroma of stew filled the kitchen and Audrey forgot all about the curtains and the coloured tablecloth. Over by the stove, Mrs Paterson slipped a large ladle from a hook and began dishing stew into bowls. The pot looked large enough to hold stew for the whole town.

She carried the bowls to the table, one at

a time. And she didn't spill one drop. As well as meat, there were potatoes, carrots and peas in the rich, dark gravy. Audrey's mouth watered. It was bad manners to start eating before everyone was seated, but Mrs Paterson moved as slowly as a wet hen.

Douglas slobbered on his thumb. Audrey tried to ignore the juicy sound.

The kitchen was growing darker. Audrey stifled a yawn. Her legs still felt as though they were shaking from the rattling cart. That morning, like the previous seven, her family had woken with the birds. All the birds in the bush had called out to each other as the sun rose.

Mrs Paterson's black skirt rustled as she reached up to tug at a cord that dangled from the ceiling. Instantly, a light came on.

Audrey gasped. Douglas forgot about his thumb. Even Price looked surprised.

'It's a miroolcool,' said Audrey.

'I beg your pardon?' Mrs Paterson blinked rapidly.

Audrey wondered if Mrs Paterson begged pardon because she couldn't think of anything else to say.

Mum smiled. 'The children have never seen an electric light. We use kerosene lanterns.'

'Of course. There is a windmill out the back, attached to a generator which gives me electricity.' With both hands, Mrs Paterson smoothed the back of her skirt before she sat at the table.

Audrey didn't understand what wind had to do with the bright light in the kitchen. But she was thrilled to see it.

'However . . .' Mrs Paterson stared across the table at Audrey. 'That is no reason to speak frivolously about things in the Good Book.'

Audrey had no idea what the word starting with 'friv' meant, but she liked books.

'Do you have *Martin Rattler*?' she asked. 'Fair dinkum, that's a *good* book. It's my favourite. Axshu ... act-u-ally ... it's my *only* book, but even if it wasn't, it would still be the best. It's got the sea in it. That's a big water they have at Adelaide and, if you stand on the beach part, you can't even see the end of it. You can hop in a boat and sail right to the edge, 'cept there is no edge. Mum says the world's round, so if a country didn't get in your way, you could sail around in a big circle, but you wouldn't fall off.'

Mrs Paterson's eyeballs wobbled.

'I'm hungwy.' Douglas grabbed his spoon.

Mrs Paterson cleared her throat. 'First, we must give thanks.'

'Fanks.' Douglas dipped into his stew.

'I mean thank the Lord. I am only the cook.' Mrs Paterson bowed her head to give her own kind of thanks.

Audrey looked down at her bowl. She was hungry enough to eat a goanna between two slabs of bark. Reluctantly she closed one eye, but kept the other open. She could hear the telltale drone of a blowfly. There it was—hovering near her plate. Fat and black. At home the Barlows kept their meat in a cool safe with hessian walls. If blowflies sneaked in, the meat became infested with wriggling, white maggots.

Audrey waved her fingers above her plate.

Mrs Paterson was grateful for a lot of things. She was taking a long time to say 'Thanks'.

The fly dived towards Audrey's stew. She waved harder. The fly changed direction and headed for Douglas's plate. Audrey couldn't call out to warn him. And although he still clutched his spoon, his eyes were clamped shut. Audrey reached out to wave her right hand over her brother's plate, while still moving her left above her own.

Finally Mrs Paterson got to a part about 'safe journey' and 'new friends'. She said 'Amen' and looked around the table.

Mum whispered a reply. Dad cleared his

throat. Price made a sound but it was hard to tell what it was. Since he turned twelve, he grunted a lot. Price reckoned it made him sound like a man. Audrey reckoned it made him sound like a camel.

Douglas shovelled in his first mouthful. Holding onto his spoon had given him a headstart.

'What do you say, little boy?' Mrs Paterson raised one eyebrow.

'More?'

'That is not the word I had in mind.' Mrs Paterson sighed and looked at Audrey, hoping for better things. 'What do you say, miss?'

Audrey looked down at her stew and flinched. 'Maggots.'

Seven

In the darkness, Audrey felt her way along the side of the iron bed. It wasn't that special having electricity if you couldn't use it. There was a candle and matches on a small table, but only in case Audrey or Douglas needed to visit the dunny out the back of the house.

Audrey's cousin, Jimmy, reckoned some people in big cities poured water down their dunnies. But Mrs Paterson had a long-drop, the same as the Barlows had at home. The seat was smoother wood, but underneath it was still only a hole in the ground. Although Mrs Paterson's dunny did have little squares of newspaper on a hook. You could sit in there and read the words.

Carefully, Audrey raised the bedroom window. She shivered as the cold night air seeped in.

Audrey scrunched down on her knees and whispered, 'Stumpy! Come here.'

A breeze stirred the leaves. Something rattled. There was no moonlight, so she couldn't see Stumpy. But she heard his footsteps, followed by his breathing.

She listened to what he had to say, then replied, 'I don't like it here. Mrs Paterson makes me think of dried plums . . .'

Audrey's eyes widened as she heard rustling, then shuffling footsteps down the hallway. A light flickered along the wall opposite the door. Shadows twisted like eerie fingers. Then came tapping on the wall.

Ghosts wandered in old houses like this when they were bored with graveyards. Audrey's heart raced.

'Cooee,' she heard, as soft as a sigh.

Her shoulders slumped with relief. She'd recognise that *cooee* anywhere.

Dad tiptoed into the room, holding a candle. He put one finger to his lips, then quietly closed the door. 'I guessed you were still awake, Two-Bob.'

She pushed the window down. It squealed on its sash. 'I think things, even when I don't want to, and it keeps me awake.'

'Hop into bed.'

'Colder than a polar bear's behind, isn't it, Dad?'

His lips twitched. 'Something like that.'

Dad placed the candle on the bedside table and looked down at Douglas. 'He's certainly the champion snorer of the Barlow family.'

Audrey climbed into bed and Dad pulled the heavy grey blankets up to her chin. He hunkered down on the floor, his face close to Audrey's. Shadows blackened his eye sockets.

'Dad, do you believe in ghosts?'

'Only the ones in our heads.'

Audrey gasped. 'Ghosts can live in people's heads? Is that because they don't have any themselves?'

'I mean that our memories, the things we think about, can sometimes haunt us.'

Audrey nodded. She didn't quite understand, but she wanted Dad to think she did. 'Do you reckon ghosts can see Stumpy?'

Dad shrugged. 'I came to say goodbye, Two-Bob. Price and I are leaving before the sun comes up.'

'Can't Mum and Douglas and me come with you? I've never been dogging.'

'Mum needs a rest. She's very tired. And I have to work. No dingoes—no money.'

Audrey thought about her mum's strained face during the trip from up north. But staying in this house for a whole month seemed impossible. 'Mrs Paterson doesn't like me.'

'She doesn't *know* you. When she does, she'll like you. Just as everyone else does.'

'But I said *maggots* at the table. I don't think Mrs Paterson says maggots at the table.'

'You won't do it again, will you?'

'But there are lots of words. What if there's another one I say by mistake? Mrs Paterson's mouth will do this.' Audrey pouted, her lips forming a knot of wrinkles.

Dad cleared his throat. 'She's not used to children, that's all. We don't have the money to stay at the hotel, and Mrs Paterson volunteered to take you in. Remember, there's a good side to everyone, Two-Bob.'

'All right,' said Audrey. 'I'll stay and look after Mum. I'll even remind her to clean her teeth.'

'You might not need to go that far.' Dad's eyes twinkled in the candlelight. 'There are other children to play with in town. And it's only for a month.'

'Stumpy will help,' said Audrey.

'I'm sure he will. But it would be better to leave him outside. I have a feeling Mrs Paterson wouldn't take kindly to your camel trotting through her house.'

'I s'pose staying here is better than a poke in the eye with a sharp stick,' she said. 'But only a bit.'

There was so much to see in Beltana.

Eight

Excited, but a little nervous, Audrey slipped her hand into her mum's. Douglas, on Mum's other side, swung her arm like a rope. In daylight, things didn't seem as gloomy as they had the night before. Audrey missed Dad and Price already. But there was so much to see in Beltana and all day to explore.

Some buildings, like the police station, schoolhouse and hotel were solidly built. But others looked as though a strong wind might blow them over. One house they passed was made of hessian bags stitched together.

Every road led somewhere—to more roads, buildings or people. Up north, the tracks near the Barlows' house led only into the bush. It wasn't often that someone turned up on those tracks.

Audrey looked up at the sky. Thick clouds skidded overhead. Everything was fast in town, even the clouds.

A truck rattled by, stirring up more dust. Audrey blinked grit from her eyes. Apart from a couple of fenced gardens, there were few bushes or grasses to keep down the dust. Every movement or puff of wind sent it flying.

An Afghan in a turban and flowing clothes led a string of camels through the dust left behind by the truck. He didn't blink or turn his head. Audrey was impressed with the straightness of his back.

On the hotel verandah a man with dark patches on his jacket leant against a pole. A wide hat-brim shielded his face. He clutched a glass as though it was stuck to his hand.

A short woman with a basket over one arm stopped to talk. When she smiled it was like the sun coming out. 'Good morning.'

'It *is* a good morning. Fair dinkum,' said Audrey. 'We're going to the store! Mum says it's got *everything* in there, even lollies. We might not be able to buy any, but we can look at them all.'

The woman laughed. She had a square-shaped face and a flat nose. Because she was almost as wide as she was tall, she looked square all over.

'New in town, are you?' she asked.

'Yes,' said Audrey's mum. 'We arrived last night ...'

'My dad says we come from the other side of the black stump,' Audrey explained, without waiting for Mum to finish her sentence. 'Where the wind starts.'

Mum squeezed her fingers.

'I'm hurrying today. My little 'un has the croup. My name's Hilda Jenkins. Drop in any time. We're just past the schoolhouse. There'll be children out the front of our place, squabbling.'

'How do you know?' asked Audrey.

'There's ten of them. So there's always something to squabble about.'

Mum's fingers twitched against Audrey's again. Audrey looked up. Her mum had an odd stare, yet she didn't seem to be focusing on anything.

'Me and Bert, my husband, we like kids,' added Mrs Jenkins. 'We're as happy as a box of birds.'

Audrey figured that was good luck. If they didn't like children, they'd have to put them in the paddock like cattle, then round them up at night for bed.

'Only hard part, except for feeding the blighters, is finding names for them all,' confided Mrs Jenkins. 'When number eight was born, we couldn't settle on a name.

36

So we called the baby "Boy". We could agree that he was definitely a *boy*.'

Mum suddenly dropped Audrey's hand, crumpled onto the dusty ground and lay still.

Douglas wailed, 'Mum's dead.'

Nine

Douglas threw himself down and held onto Mum with both arms.

'Move aside, dear. I can't help if you get in the way,' said Mrs Jenkins.

Audrey gently detached Douglas. She picked him up and sat him on her hip. He clung to her like a sack of wheat on a hook.

Mrs Jenkins knelt beside Mum, then she placed her fingers under Mum's chin.

'She's not dead, little fella,' said Mrs Jenkins, breathlessly. 'She has a pulse. That means her heart is beating, and her hands just moved.'

'Are you sure?' Audrey's own heart was beating loud enough for both her *and* Mum.

The man from the hotel verandah joined them. He seemed to move slowly, yet he reached them in no time at all. Then he hovered, not sure what to do.

A woman in a green dress, her hands fluttering like an impatient butterfly, left her front yard to scurry over. Her eyes darted here and there, showing that her thoughts were fluttering as much as her hands.

Mum muttered, but made no sense.

'She's all right, Dougie,' Audrey told her brother. 'She made a noise.'

Mum opened her eyes and tried to sit up.

Mrs Jenkins slid one arm around her back to support her. 'Don't try to stand. Sit still.'

She looked up at the woman with the fluttering hands. 'Sylvia, would you go and let the sisters at the hospital know we're coming?'

Sylvia scuttled away, her hands moving faster than her feet.

'I've got the horses and dray just there,' said the man from the hotel verandah.

Mrs Jenkins, solid and calm, nodded. 'We'll take her to get her checked.'

She was good at telling people what to do. A mother of so many children would have lots of practice.

'I don't want to go.' Mum struggled to push the helping hands away. Her voice was faint, but her words were now clear. 'My children need me ...'

Audrey trembled. She tried to stop it, so she wouldn't scare Douglas even more. It didn't help that he had his arms wrapped tightly around her neck. She was starting to feel dizzy herself. With one hand, she eased his grip. 'It's all right, Dougie. Mum's sitting up.'

Douglas buried his face in her neck.

'I'll see to the children.' Mrs Jenkins looked at Audrey. 'Where are you staying?'

Audrey couldn't think of anything but Mum's blank stare and the thumping of her own heart. Then she said, 'With ... um ... Mrs Pating ... Paterson.'

'Paterson's curse,' said the man. He blushed and his whole face turned as red as his nose. 'Sorry ... slip of the tongue.'

Mrs Jenkins glared at him. 'Norm, if you spent less time bending your elbow at the pub, you might find your brain worked at the same time as your mouth.'

Head down, he sloped off to get his horses and dray.

Maybe the red-faced man had been joking. But Audrey felt cold fingers dance down her spine. If Mum was kept in the hospital by the sisters, she and Douglas would be alone with Mrs Paterson. Audrey knew about the weed called Paterson's curse. It was poisonous.

Ten

Heat from Mrs Paterson's wood oven warmed Audrey's back. 'I want to come to the hospital too,' she said.

A picture of Mum crumpling onto the dusty footpath kept flashing into her mind. The last hour had been a blur of unfamiliar faces: Mrs Jenkins, the man with the red nose and Sylvia with the fluttering hands.

Audrey patted her little brother on the shoulder.

Mrs Paterson folded her hands. 'I *beg* your pardon?'

Audrey hesitated, not sure what this particular *beg your pardon* was about.

Mrs Paterson sighed. 'I want to come, *please.*'

'I want to come too, *please,*' repeated Audrey in her politest voice.

'No, I'm sorry. You cannot.'

'But you just made me say *please.*' A knot formed in Audrey's stomach.

'Manners are not permission.' Mrs Paterson made a shooing motion.

'Dad said I have to look after Mum.'

'A hospital is not the place for children. They carry germs. The sisters won't let you in.' Mrs Paterson placed a black hat on her grey hair and slid in a long pin to hold it in place. 'I will visit your mother and report back.'

'But you don't love her,' Audrey burst out.

'I know how to do my duty.' Mrs Paterson hooked a handbag over her right arm.

Duty was one of those tricky words that seemed to be one thing but was really another. And it didn't sound good.

Mrs Paterson walked from the kitchen into the dim hallway.

Audrey and Douglas followed her.

'Are you sure you don't know where your father is?' Mrs Paterson stopped beside the open sitting room door.

Audrey shook her head. 'He follows the dingoes. Although sometimes *they* follow *him*. At night they sneak into his camp to eat his boots.'

'I hope I can trust you children alone here till I return,' said Mrs Paterson.

'I've got Stumpy,' said Audrey, without thinking.

'Who?'

Audrey covered her mouth with one hand. She hadn't meant to speak about Stumpy. But now that she had, it was best to tell the truth. Mrs Paterson would sniff out a made-up story in a second. Besides, Stumpy was Audrey's friend. She wasn't going to tell fibs about him.

'Stumpy's my camel. He's outside. Dad said he could stay but I wasn't to let him run through the house.'

Douglas wriggled from Audrey's grasp and scooted out the door into the over-grown garden, where there were good hiding places and no snappy voices.

Mrs Paterson's eyebrows stretched up into the shade of her hat-brim. 'If you tell lies, you'll grow pimples on your tongue.'

'Stumpy's my camel, all right, but he's invisible.'

There was a long pause where all Audrey could hear was the ticking of the clock on the sitting room mantelpiece. *Tick-tock, tick-tock*. Each swing of the pendulum seemed louder than the last.

'There's no such thing as an invisible camel.' Mrs Paterson's voice was as sharp as tin. 'He's imaginary.'

'He's *not* imaginary. He's real. But not everyone can see him.'

'Nonsense.'

'Don't you believe in things you can't see?' asked Audrey.

'Of course not. No sensible person would.'

'But people dream. And you can't see that.'

'Someone sees it. The dreamer.'

''Zactly,' said Audrey. 'Someone can see Stumpy. *Me.*'

Eleven

Audrey stood alone in the sitting room. Dougie was still in the garden and Stumpy had sulked off somewhere. Mrs Paterson had hurt his feelings when she said he wasn't real.

With the curtains drawn, the room was gloomy. The air was stuffy. White cloth covered the arms and backs of the chairs. A faded red carpet square covered the floorboards, except for a strip around the edge of the room. The only sound was the ticking of the clock.

Before Mrs Paterson left, she had recited a long list of what to do and what not to do. Mostly 'Don'ts', with a few 'Do's' that were boring. Audrey couldn't remember most of them. She hoped that as long as she didn't break anything, Mrs Paterson wouldn't be too fussy.

Fresh air wouldn't be on anyone's 'Don't' list. Audrey's mum always said fresh air made people strong and healthy. Which was a good thing, because back home they had no glass in their windows. Audrey tucked back the curtains and lifted the window. A breeze trickled in. Specks of dust danced along the beam of sunlight.

She saw Douglas at the side of the house, jumping about like a newborn lamb. Usually he liked pretending to be a bird. But Audrey had never seen a bird hop like that.

The day before, Audrey couldn't keep a lid on her excitement. But already, after only one night, she longed to go home. Her house had no fancy curtains or proper floors like Mrs Paterson's did, but it was friendly.

'I'll distractionate myself,' whispered Audrey. She nodded, pleased with such a good idea and a difficult word like 'distractionate'.

The red-nosed man, Norm, had called Mrs Paterson a 'curse'. But Audrey's dad had said there was a good side to everyone. So there must be one in Mrs Paterson. Audrey decided to look for it.

She thought hard.

Mrs Paterson was letting them stay in her house. That wasn't completely good, but Audrey had to start somewhere.

She spun round, looking for ideas, and spotted a wooden bookcase. The old lady liked books, especially 'good' ones.

Carefully, Audrey ran her finger along each spine. They were probably books for grown-ups with long words. But Audrey hoped there might be pictures. She chose a book, opened it, then lifted it to her face and sniffed. The paper had a fresh, woody aroma.

At home, Audrey kept *Martin Rattler* and her diary in a tin under her bed. The tin kept out termites. They thought books were yummy food. Termites didn't care about important words. All they thought about were their termite tummies.

Memories of home made Audrey feel itchy. She frowned, then turned a page of Mrs Paterson's book and found a drawing of a gully with rocks each side.

Outside, Douglas squealed.

Audrey jumped.

Then she heard another sound that sent her running down the hallway.

Twelve

Mrs Paterson's garden was full of goats. *Starving* goats. Douglas jumped up and down, clapping his hands.

'We have to get them out,' shouted Audrey. 'Dougie, that goat's eating the grey bush ...' Her sentence ended in a squeal. She dashed forward to grab the goat as it ripped off a branch, leaving a bitter smell from the crushed leaves. The goat trotted away with the branch in its mouth.

There were seven goats, but it seemed like many more.

'Dougie, go round that way,' said Audrey, shooing goats towards the gate. Two shot out onto the road.

The others found something better to do. One took a mouthful of the ivy and tore it from the wall. Tiny black marks were left behind from its suckers. Audrey grabbed the nearest goat and shoved its rump. Bleating a protest, it gradually moved towards the open gate. The goat smelled like old cheese. Audrey gave one last heave and the goat was out. She clanged the gate shut behind it.

The evicted goat bleated even louder. It was still hungry, and now it was annoyed. It reared up, hooking its front legs on the gate, as it scrabbled to climb over. Audrey hoped the gate was stronger than the goat.

But the next goat in Mrs Paterson's garden was not so easy to grab. It danced to one side and then the other whenever Audrey came close. She started to panic.

The only part of Douglas that moved was

his jaw. It bounced up and down as he sucked on his thumb.

There was a flash of movement to Audrey's right as something jumped over the gate into the garden.

But it wasn't a goat. It was a boy in grey shorts.

Audrey glimpsed dark eyelashes above freckled cheeks. As though he had springs on his feet, the boy leapt lightly onto the back of the nearest goat.

'Open the gate!' he yelled.

Audrey was quick to obey.

The boy leant forward, one hand on each side of the goat, and nudged it with his knees and heels. He rode the goat with the same skill that a drover would ride a horse. The goat ran out onto the dusty footpath to join its hairy friends.

Flustered, Audrey aimed a look down the road. If Mrs Paterson came back and the goats were still in the garden, there'd be big trouble.

He rubbed his nose on the back of his hand.

Thirteen

Far sooner than Audrey expected, the garden was goat-free.

Douglas's bottom lip quivered.

'It's all right, Dougie,' said Audrey. 'They've gone.'

'I don't wike goats now.'

'I like *eating* them,' teased the boy.

A little shorter than Audrey, he had an uneven and very short haircut. He must have wriggled while it was being cut or else his mother had saved time by doing two haircuts at once. A curved scar marked his chin and his brown eyes were flecked with yellow.

As though he guessed Audrey's thoughts about his haircut, he said, 'Just had me ears lowered.'

Suddenly shy, she shrugged, as though she hadn't been thinking about that at all.

'I'm Boy.'

'Oh. You're the boy, *Boy*. I mean, the boy *called* Boy.'

'Sounds like stuttering, doesn't it?' He rubbed his nose on the back of his hand. 'Me brother Hughie's got a real stutter. When he's excited he calls me "B . . . B . . . Boy". Which is a lot of *B*'s.' Boy slid the back of his hand down the right leg of his grey shorts. 'Mum sent me down to see if you're all right.'

Audrey wiped perspiration from her forehead. 'You won't say anything about the goats . . .'

'Heck no! The old lady could pin your ears back with that voice of hers. My dad reckons she broke a glass once just by raising her voice when she was cross.'

Audrey swallowed with difficulty. At home, she was sometimes in trouble. But no one shouted.

'I'm takin' a goat home for the pot.' Boy nodded towards the goats, which had moved down the road, but were still milling around searching for lunch. 'I can catch 'em real quick. I catch rabbits too, with my hands. You just have to know which way to run. They kind of zigzag.' He gestured with one grubby hand to show Audrey the path a fleeing rabbit would take.

'Don't the goats belong to somebody?'

Boy shook his head. 'There's hundreds of 'em. The explorers brought 'em because they were food that could walk by itself. But they didn't eat 'em all. Now the goats run all over the place. The police station's got a sign that tells goats to keep out. Goats can't read so they get into the horse paddock anyway and eat the grass.' His eyes sparkled.

'I'm hungwy,' interrupted Douglas.

Audrey knelt beside him, one finger against her lips in a shushing gesture. 'You mustn't tell Mrs Paterson about the goats. It's a secret. You like secrets, don't you?'

Sometimes Douglas opened his mouth and words burst out by themselves. No one in the family paid too much attention. But Audrey had a feeling that Mrs Paterson would.

From behind them, came the squeak of a hinge.

'What is going on here?' said a voice that cut like a knife.

Mrs Paterson stood by the gate, one eyebrow raised. She seemed to use her eyebrow instead of words quite a lot. Right now, that brow looked annoyed.

'We got a seecwet,' said Douglas.

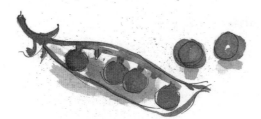

Fourteen

'It's a game we're playing,' explained Audrey. 'While we ... um ... do some gardening for you.'

It was true, in a way, except that all the gardening had been done by goats, not by Audrey or Douglas.

'Do you have permission to touch my garden?'

Douglas slipped his hand into Audrey's.

'Not really,' said Audrey. 'But the weeds will choke your nice plants.'

'I believe I gave strict instructions that

you were only to play in the side part of the garden.'

Audrey couldn't think of a single thing to say. That didn't happen very often. And when it did, she was surprised.

'I saw goats when I turned the corner.' Mrs Paterson sounded suspicious.

'I was tryin' to catch one, Mrs P,' said Boy. 'Good tucker if you get one that's not too old and you cook 'em long enough.' He jammed his hands into his pockets.

'Mrs *Paterson*. Your abbreviation makes me sound like a legume.'

'What?'

'A pea or bean,' said Audrey. She often helped her mum in the vegetable garden at home, which meant she knew all kinds of gardening things. Like the meaning of legume. That tomatoes and potatoes shouldn't be planted together because they were cousins. And that it didn't work if you stuffed a plant back in the ground and pretended you hadn't ripped it out by mistake. The plant always shrivelled.

Thinking of home and her mother made Audrey feel like someone had pinched her right where her heart was beating. 'Did you see Mum, Mrs Paterson?'

'Mum!' said Douglas, as though he was calling her.

Audrey rubbed his back with the flat of her hand.

'Yes, I saw her. Come inside.' Mrs Paterson aimed her eagle eyes at Boy. 'You may go home, young Jenkins.'

'Boy,' he said quietly.

'I can see you are a boy. I am no spring chicken, but I am not blind yet.'

'My *name* is Boy.'

'Oh, you're *that* Jenkins. There are so many of you.'

Boy nodded. 'Mum says we all look the same, too, 'cept we're different sizes. Peas in a pod. Don't feel bad about forgettin' me name, Mrs Paterson. Dad forgets too. He calls us by number. I'm eight.'

He pulled a folded sheet of paper from the pocket of his grey shorts. 'Mum sent you a note.'

Mrs Paterson took it with two fingers. 'You didn't read it, did you?'

'I couldn't. And I tried real hard. Looks like a fly crawled across the page. Not many people can read Mum's writin'. I don't reckon she can neither. She just remembers what she wrote.'

'Boy Jenkins, looking at your mother's note to me is highly improper. Go on now.' The old lady strode along the path towards the door, her starched skirt rustling around her thin ankles.

Douglas and Audrey, hand in hand, followed close behind.

Audrey tried to think of something nice to say that might melt the stern look on the old lady's face. 'I'm glad you're not blind yet, Mrs Paterson, even though you're really old.'

Fifteen

Mrs Paterson strode into the sitting room. The wrinkles on her forehead bunched up like the ridges on a washboard. 'My window. It's *open*. How do you explain that, Audrey Barlow?'

'The room smelt funny. I let some fresh air in for you. And the sunshine looks pretty.'

Mrs Paterson marched across the room. She pushed back the net curtains, closed the window with a snap, then half-closed the heavier curtains. Audrey's spirits dulled with the room.

'Sunlight fades carpet,' said Mrs Paterson.

Audrey looked down at the floor. The threadbare carpet square was already faded.

'Obviously my instructions fell on blocked ears. I see that you have a problem with remembering things. Do *not* enter this room without permission.'

Douglas resumed sucking his thumb.

'Stop that,' commanded Mrs Paterson. 'Thumb-sucking is for babies. And your teeth will grow crooked.'

Douglas didn't take out his thumb. Though he *did* stop slurping, which was some improvement.

Mrs Paterson sat in a high-backed arm-chair without removing the white covers. She held herself so stiffly that she seemed in danger of snapping a bone. 'You may sit.'

Audrey perched on the edge of the two-seater sofa. Mum would call it a 'lounge'. Audrey raised one eyebrow, just the way Mrs Paterson did, to show she was listening.

Douglas stood beside Audrey, jiggling his legs.

Audrey's palms were damp but she didn't dare wipe them.

Mrs Paterson reached up and unpinned her hat, then placed it on her knees. 'Your mother has instructed me to tell you she is in a certain condition.'

Audrey frowned. 'In the hospital?'

'Yes, she is staying at the hospital.'

'Hostibool,' repeated Douglas.

'What's wrong with Mum that she's in the hospital condition?' asked Audrey. 'Is her leg bad?'

'No worse than usual, I believe. But I don't think you quite understand my meaning. By *condition*, I mean that your family will, in the course of time, grow larger.'

Audrey was confused. 'Is Mum getting fatter?'

Douglas threw himself across Audrey's knees.

Mrs Paterson went pink. Her fingers fiddled with the brim of her black hat. Audrey thought it was strange. Mrs Paterson didn't seem a fidgety sort of person.

'You will notice some changes . . .' Mrs Patterson took a deep breath. 'Your mother is expecting.'

'What is she expecting, Mrs Paterson?'

'A *baby*. Your mother is expecting a baby. Do you understand?'

'Oh, that's what it is. I watched Sassafras squeeze out Buttons.'

The pink on Mrs Paterson's face deepened to red. 'You watched . . .?' Her voiced cracked and her words fell into the gap.

'Sassafras is our mother goat. Her baby is called Buttons, because she is cute as a button.'

'Sassafwas eats eveyfing,' said Douglas. 'Me too. I'm hungwy.'

'When is Mum leaving the hospital?' asked Audrey.

'I do not know. Things are not quite right. She has to stay for a while. Perhaps several weeks.'

'*Weeks?*' Audrey felt her face go hot. That sometimes happened before she cried. But she was determined not to cry today. Not in front of Mrs Paterson. And not in front of her little brother. He might be scared. Certainly, he would cry too. 'What . . . what about me and Dougie?'

'You will stay with me.'

Audrey wished her family had never come to town.

She sat on the sofa, her hands clasped lightly in her lap.

Sixteen

Audrey's lunch was leftover stewed meat between thick slices of bakery bread. It felt like a solid lump in her stomach. Normally she would have loved every mouthful. But not today.

She sat on the sofa, her hands clasped lightly in her lap.

'Do try not to slouch, child,' said Mrs Paterson. 'Else your back will bend like a horseshoe.'

Audrey had never seen anyone whose back looked like a horseshoe. But what Mrs

Paterson said was probably true. She was old and had seen more backs than anyone.

A tickle began on the end of Audrey's nose. She tried to think of something else, *anything* else, rather than scratch it.

Mrs Paterson looked over her round glasses. 'Ladies sit still. They do not wiggle their lower limbs.'

Audrey held her legs still and wondered if proper ladies felt as bored as she did. She looked up at the shiny brown clock on the mantelpiece. Its ticking could be heard right through the house. The clock didn't have proper numbers, just lines, V's and X's. Maybe it was one of those 'two-bob' clocks that Bloke had talked about.

'Mrs Paterson, why doesn't your clock have numbers?'

'It *has* numbers. They are in Latin. They are usually called Roman numerals.'

'We only have Australian words in our house,' said Audrey. 'We don't know how to do Latin.'

'I am sure you do not. In any case, it is a dead language.'

Audrey blinked. Why would Mrs Paterson have dead numbers on her clock?

'Do you think ghosts can read dead numbers? That'd help if they were supposed to come out at exactly midnight.'

'Tommyrot.'

'Thank you.'

'That was not intended as a compliment.'

Audrey fiddled with the end of her plait. Although she was tempted to chew on it, she decided to let it drop. Price said that chewing your hair gave you a hairy chest.

She longed for Douglas to wake up from his nap. He would totter out with sweaty, mussed-up hair and a confused expression. His thumb would be in his mouth. Audrey glanced down the hallway, but it was empty. The rumble of snores from the end bedroom told her that he was sound asleep.

Stumpy was still hiding. He was probably

scared. This house wasn't much fun for a camel like him.

'You may begin writing your list of house rules now,' said Mrs Paterson. 'It might aid your memory. Although the school is closed for the holidays, you should keep up your skills.'

'I don't have any skills,' said Audrey. 'But I can write words. Not big ones. But they're proper words.'

She picked up the pencil and paper from the small table beside her. 'Do you think people are the same as the list?'

'Whatever do you mean?' said Mrs Paterson.

'I reckon there might be "Do" and "Don't" sorts of people. If you're born a "Don't", you can't help it. You just see "Don'ts" everywhere.'

Mrs Paterson's mouth drooped.

Audrey wondered if Mrs Paterson ever laughed. Audrey's home up north was small and there was nothing fancy about it.

But her family laughed a lot. Sometimes at each other. Sometimes at themselves. And sometimes at nothing at all.

Here, the old house was large and there was a lace tablecloth on the sitting room table. But the clock had dead numbers and the rooms were filled with shadows.

Seventeen

Mrs Paterson made a *click-clack* sound as she knitted with her wooden needles. The yarn wriggled and the needles wobbled and somehow it was all growing into a red something-or-other.

'That Jenkins family,' said Mrs Paterson, 'I'm not certain they are suitable company.'

Audrey held her breath. Mrs Jenkins's note had asked if Audrey and Douglas could come over to play with her children. Audrey wanted to go. She *needed* to go. It was part of the secret plan she was hatching.

'They have ... foibles.' Mrs Paterson tossed her head like a sulky horse.

'What's a foydool?'

'F-o-i-b-l-e.' Mrs Paterson spelt out the word. 'It's a bad habit. Those children run wild and they always have runny noses.'

Boy *had* wiped his nose with the back of his hand, and then hidden the evidence on the side of his shorts. Audrey didn't care about that. Camels often had runny noses. Sometimes they snotted on purpose to annoy people. Stumpy didn't do that, though.

'There are *some* girls amongst that brood. Mrs Jenkins herself is a good-hearted woman. And it is a duty to be kind to the poor. Faith, hope and charity.'

'Are they the names of the girls?'

Mrs Paterson made a *tsk* sound. 'They are the three great virtues.'

'Is virtue like washing dishes?' asked Audrey.

'I would say so.' Mrs Paterson tugged on her knitting yarn.

So it's a bad thing, decided Audrey. But she didn't say that aloud.

'We *could* consider it part of your social instruction. And I can't be expected to keep two children amused all day long.'

Mrs Paterson was so old she had most likely forgotten how to play.

Audrey studied the mantelpiece above the fireplace. There were several pretty plates, a small vase holding stalks of lavender and two old photographs. The men in the photos looked alike, although the older man had a crooked nose.

Mrs Paterson held up the red rectangle. 'This should fit *you*.'

'Where would my arms go?'

'I have not reached that far yet.' Mrs Paterson's eyebrow did its jump. 'Don't you know how to knit, child?'

'Mum tried to show me once. But I was little and the stitches kept dropping off the sticks. It was too hard.'

'They are *needles*, not sticks.' Mrs Paterson

peered over the top of her metal-framed glasses. 'It's high time you learnt. Come and watch over my shoulder.'

Audrey put down her pencil and paper. Knitting might be a 'Do' that was fun. She could make something warm for Dad to wear when he camped out bush.

Close up, Mrs Paterson smelt like baby powder. She didn't smell old. Although Audrey wasn't sure what *old* was supposed to smell like. Potatoes didn't smell too good when they got wrinkly and started to sprout. But potatoes were not the same as people.

'This is how you hold the needles. You rest each one on the part of your hand between your thumb and forefinger and you do this . . .' Mrs Paterson twiddled the needles and a stitch appeared.

'That's like magic.'

'Magic is an instrument of the Devil. So is card-playing. This is simply knotting yarn with two needles.'

Audrey wondered why a devil would want to play cards.

'Here's how I learnt to knit when I was young,' said Mrs Paterson.

Audrey sneaked a look at her grey hair and the wrinkles on her long neck. It was hard to imagine her being a little girl. But she wasn't born with her hair in a bun or her heart in a cage.

'In through the bunny hole ...' Mrs Paterson inserted the right needle into the first loop on the left needle. 'Around the big tree.' She wound the yarn between the two needles. 'Back through the bunny hole.' The right needle came back across the middle loop. 'And off hops he.' Mrs Paterson pulled the new loop of yarn from the left to the right needle.

'Of course, I can't give you needles while you're learning. You might break them. You can start with nails. There are some long ones out in the shed.'

'Nails won't make the right sound,' said

Audrey, half-expecting an abrupt reply.

But instead, Mrs Paterson slowly nodded. 'You are quite right. I practised knitting with nails in the outside toilet on Sundays when I was your age. My father was a good man, but strict. He believed the Sabbath should be rigidly enforced. No activity of any kind.'

'I practise reading in *your* dunny,' said Audrey.

The old lady lowered her eyelids. 'Of course what I did was deceitful. I do not approve of such behaviour now that I know better.'

'Who are those people in the photos on the mantelpiece?'

Mrs Paterson's hands stopped making bunny holes and sending yarn around big trees. 'Hasn't anyone taught you that asking questions of grown-ups is rude?'

'I don't think so. I'd remember something like that.'

'You have been in the bush too long. It's a disgrace.' Mrs Paterson stabbed her needles into the ball of wool. 'You, child, are going to be my next project. Let us see if we can shake the bush dust from your manners and turn you into a lady.'

Audrey felt her heart sink into her shoes.

Dear Mum

I wrote the top of this letter like you showed me and
the numbers are real ones. See? Not like the dead
ones on the clock.

Hope you are having a good rest. Me and Dougie
miss you. Xx. That was two kisses, one ~~form~~ from
each of us.

Mrs Paterson is teaching us to do good manners
at the ~~tabel~~ table. So far we learned—

Don't sing when you are eating. (You'd spit on
the table.)

Don't put your head down to your bowl. Bring the
spoon up to your mouth. (When I told Mrs Paterson
that lifting the spoon makes splashes on the tablecloth
she said that King George would never put his head
down to the bowl so we carnt neither. But I don't think
she has really seen the King.)

Mrs Paterson says Stumpy is a lie. Which is
anuther lie. She reckons I'm not aloud to say he is
real. But if I say he's not then that is a lie too. So I
got some thinking to work that one out. Stumpy is not
here much. He knows Mrs Paterson doesn't like him.

My hand is hurting so I will stop now.

Before I go to sleep I will say goodnight to you,
Dad and Price. Even tho you carnt hear me. That's why
I told you.

Love from Audrey, Dougie and Stumpy

Eighteen

Audrey lay in the dark. The third night in Mrs Paterson's house was no easier than the first. Back home, she knew all the sounds. Even the tiny feet that sometimes ran across the roof didn't bother her. Possums were naughty but fun.

As hard as Audrey listened, she couldn't hear Stumpy outside. The first camel-breeding station in Australia was only a few miles away, so Stumpy was probably out there making friends.

Mrs Paterson's house seemed to *breathe*.

'Audwey,' whispered Douglas from the other bed.

'Yes?'

'I want to go home now.'

It was a perfect sentence, the longest one Audrey had heard her little brother say.

'We can't leave Mum here at the hospital on her own, can we?' said Audrey.

Something scratched at the window.

'Wossat?' asked Douglas.

'Twigs from that tree outside the window, moving in the wind.'

It was the right thing to say. The kind of thing Mum would say, but Audrey didn't sound nearly as confident.

The scratching came again. Leaves shaking in the wind sounded like whispering.

Audrey called out, 'Mrs Paterson.'

There was no answer.

'Mrs Paterson!'

A light came on down the hallway. Audrey heard Mrs Paterson's slippers scuffing the linoleum. Then she appeared in the doorway, wrapped in a dressing-gown that was as dark as her daytime clothes.

'What is the matter?'

Audrey turned onto her side. 'Can me and Dougie have the light on?' Then she added '*please*', remembering how fond of that word Mrs Paterson seemed to be.

'Have you been naughty?'

'Not 'specially. Course, sometimes I might be naughty and I don't know. So maybe that isn't really naughty. Can you be naughty if you don't know you're doing it?'

There was a pause, then Mrs Paterson's voice floated around the room like a leaf on water. 'I have not understood one word you just said. No, you may *not* have the light on all night. If you have been good, then you do not need to be afraid of the dark.'

'I'm not scared of the dark,' said Audrey. 'I'm scared of the house.'

'It is just walls and rooms.'

'This house is *sad*.'

Mrs Paterson gasped. At least, Audrey thought she did. The sound was so quiet that she couldn't be sure.

The old lady turned and walked away.

Seconds later, the light went out.

Audrey knew her dad wasn't often wrong. Yet she wondered if he had made a mistake about *everybody* having a good side.

She went across to the other bed, scooped up Douglas and carried him over to her own. He took her pillow and kicked her in the leg several times before he settled.

Audrey lay awake long after she finished telling Douglas stories about Stumpy's pranks. Long after Douglas started snoring and twitching. And long after the sound of crying had faded at the other end of the house.

Nineteen

'Make sure the water is boiling.' Mrs Paterson's voice easily reached the kitchen from the sitting room.

'I will,' Audrey called back.

She was careful, as her mum had taught her. This stove was a corker. The wood fire was inside a metal box and the kettle sat on top of it. At home, Audrey's family had only an open fire in their kitchen.

'Warm the pot first.'

'I will.' Audrey had already done it, but she didn't want to say so.

A mound of black leaves from a Griffiths Brothers Choice Tea tin sat in the pot. Was that too many? It would be too hard to dig them out. Anyway, what would she do with them? The leaves were damp and couldn't go back in the tin. Audrey added boiling water to the teapot.

'Make sure you let it draw for at least three minutes.'

'I will,' repeated Audrey.

'The tea-cosy is under the sink. Put it on so the tea doesn't go cold.'

Audrey slipped the striped, knitted tea-cosy over the pot. She struggled getting the spout into the hole but burnt her finger only once. She picked up the pot with both hands and poured tea into a cup. Tea splashed onto the saucer. The tea looked awfully dark. More like the brew a swagman would make if he left the leaves in his billy for a long time.

Audrey counted eight leaves floating in the cup. She wondered if she should have strained it. The water was too hot for her to stick her fingers in to pick out the tea leaves. And if she tried to get them with a teaspoon, she knew she'd drop them and make an even bigger mess. It was too late now. Wobbling a little, she placed the teacup and saucer on the silver tray next to the milk and sugar.

She was glad that Douglas was in the bedroom making a cubbyhouse with the blankets. Otherwise he would be running around her feet and she would be sure to trip.

'Don't forget the milk and sugar,' Mrs Paterson called again from the sitting room.

Picking up the tray, Audrey inched towards the door. More tea spilled over the side of the cup. It sat on the saucer in a lake of brown liquid. But there was still enough left in the cup for Mrs Paterson to have a drink.

When Audrey reached the sitting room table, she wasn't sure how to put the tray down. If she bent over, the remaining tea would slop out. Mrs Paterson solved her problem by taking the tray herself.

Audrey expected Mrs Paterson to tip the slopped tea from the saucer back into the cup, as Dad did. But the old lady pretended it wasn't there. She added one sugar, a dash of milk, and stirred the tea in a clockwise direction six times. Then she took a sip and coughed.

'It's not too strong, is it?' asked Audrey.

Mrs Paterson's eyes watered. 'Just a tickle in my throat. It's delicious. Thank you.'

'You have soft hands,' said Audrey, 'And none of your fingers are bent.'

Mrs Paterson made a strange noise in the back of her throat. 'Thank you. I am most fortunate in that regard. I use hand cream. And there is lanoline in the wool I knit. Another good reason to keep one's hands occupied in that way.'

'Can we ... *may* Dougie and I go to the Jenkins's now, please?' Audrey was afraid the old lady would change her mind. There was a town waiting outside the garden fence, other children to play with and a secret plan to carry out.

'You may go,' Mrs Paterson said at last. 'I would accompany you, but my arthritis is not good today. Do you know the way?'

'Yes, town is easy because the roads are straight.'

'Be back by half-past five. Keep in mind that I cannot abide anyone who is not punctual.'

'I won't punch anyone. Neither will Dougie. He doesn't like fighting.'

Mrs Paterson closed her eyes for a moment, then said, '*Punctual.* Not *punch you all.* I refer to you not being late.'

'I can do that too,' said Audrey.

The old lady narrowed her eyes. 'You are being very polite today.'

'That's because I'm your project,' said Audrey. 'And *you're* mine. I'm looking for your good side.'

Twenty

Audrey left the house with Mrs Paterson's list of 'Don'ts' for walking through town ringing in her ears. It was almost as long as the list for how to behave inside the house. Mrs Paterson had finished with, 'Don't let the Jenkins children lead you into trouble.' She had not said what kind of 'trouble'. Audrey wished she had. That might have made the list more interesting. But Mrs Paterson had rules without many ideas.

If Audrey's secret plan backfired, she knew she would get into trouble for sure.

Douglas gripped her hand firmly. His skipping tugged on her arm.

A large whirlwind sped across the road, gathering dust as Stumpy arrived.

Audrey grinned. 'You were a long time.' She understood his wanting to be with other camels because she was excited about making new friends too.

Clouds covered the sun. Audrey shivered, despite her cardigan. A breeze played with the hem of her blue smock dress. Fine rain began to tickle her face.

Beltana was rich with water. Two creeks snaked around the town. Audrey wished her family had even *one* creek near their house. But at least they had the well and, so far, it had never dried up.

A boy with flappy ears walked past. He coughed with his mouth wide open. Mrs Paterson wouldn't have liked that. You were supposed to cover your mouth when you coughed, so people couldn't see down your throat.

'Hello.' Audrey smiled at the boy.

'Hello,' repeated Douglas.

The boy didn't answer.

Douglas made a noise.

Stumpy whispered to Audrey.

'No, Stumpy,' Audrey replied. 'There's nothing wrong with Dougie. He's just humming.'

Douglas hummed louder.

Audrey's steps slowed as they walked past the hospital. She looked at each window, hoping to see a familiar face or a hand waving a handkerchief. But there was nothing. Not the slightest brush of a curtain.

There were more people in town than out bush. But more people didn't always stop you feeling lonely.

Mrs Jenkins came bustling out of the house.

Twenty-one

They passed the tiny school with its pointed roof. It was surrounded by a wire fence with wooden posts. That wouldn't keep the children in. They could squeeze through the gaps or climb over it. At home, Audrey and Price often thought of ways to avoid lessons with Mum at the kitchen table.

Audrey and Douglas reached the Jenkins's house without breaking a single Mrs Paterson-rule. Although Stumpy had come along, and Mrs Paterson wouldn't have liked that too much.

The Jenkins's house was nestled between two others. Audrey could have guessed which one it was by the sound of all the children's voices. They were raised in friendly argument. At least, she *hoped* it was friendly.

A line of scrappy bushes with more twigs than leaves divided the front and back yards. The fence was half-broken. The Jenkins's house looked small for twelve people. It was made from flattened kerosene tins, the metal sheets dented here and there. Smoke rose from the chimney. The chimney looked like the most solid part of the building.

Stumpy hung back.

'You can go and play if you want, Stumpy,' said Audrey.

He was gone in a flash.

Audrey wasn't sure about going in either. Ten was a lot of children to meet all at once. But Douglas dragged on her arm, pulling her forward. He couldn't count to ten yet, so he wasn't nervous.

As they neared the back of the house, there was a yell.

Her heart beating fast, Audrey rounded the corner. Children of varying heights stood in the backyard watching Boy. They bellowed a mixture of cheers and protests. Boy had both hands against the outside dunny and he was pushing hard. The dunny rocked back and forth. Muffled shouts came from inside.

Mrs Jenkins came bustling out of the house. 'Boy. Stop that. If you had a brain it'd be lonely.'

'Ma, he's been in there that long his head's caved in.' Then Boy looked up, saw Audrey and grinned.

Mrs Jenkins turned. 'I'm sorry ... Boy isn't usually ...' She wiped her hands on her dark green apron and shrugged. 'Actually he *is* usually up to something. But I don't always catch him at it.'

Boy started to introduce his brothers and sisters. Audrey wasn't sure she would remember so many names. They all had crooked haircuts. There wasn't a straight line on any head in the yard. The three girls wore overalls, like the boys.

'I can do this . . . look.' A short girl, about five years old, stretched her mouth to show that she had a tooth missing. Then she poked the tip of her tongue through the gap.

'Dougie do this.' He poked his right fore-finger into his ear.

Thumping came from inside the dunny. The Jenkins mob ignored it.

Boy's shirt was ripped and his grey shorts grubby. His legs were thin, with knobbly knees. Audrey was reminded of the goats back home. There was a dirty streak across Boy's left cheek.

'This is me brother, Simon, number four. Parker, number three.' Boy rattled off the names and birth orders of each child. 'Phillip doesn't like being called number two.' Boy's eyes gleamed with mischief.

More thumping from inside the dunny interrupted the list of names. Boy undid the outside latch.

A lad who was slightly older and a lot redder in the face than Boy, flew out, his hands curled into fists. 'Put up yer dooks.'

Boy shook his head. 'We got visitors.'

The red-faced boy looked at Audrey and Douglas. 'Are you the orphans?'

Audrey's felt as though she had been slapped. 'I am *not* an orphan. Neither is Dougie. Our mum's in the hospital.' But the word *orphan* made her think, for an instant, what it would feel like if Mum didn't come home.

'Liam, isn't there a pile of wood waiting to be chopped?' said Mrs Jenkins. 'You just volunteered.'

'But, Ma, it isn't my turn . . .'

Mrs Jenkins raised one arm and pointed to the side of the house. She didn't need to say anything else. Her arm said it all. 'Settle down, the lot of you.'

Boy came to stand beside Audrey. 'Ma made scones, and there's real butter. From a cow.'

Audrey realised she was hungry. She had never tasted cow butter, only goat butter, which was stinky. Mrs Paterson used dripping. She said bread and dripping had been good enough for her when she was growing up, so it was good enough for her visitors. It tasted all right. But real butter would be a treat.

Boy smiled at Audrey, his eyes switching from yellow to brown.

Audrey smiled back. Boy was cheeky, but not wicked. And he was daring, but not stupid—unless you counted rocking the dunny when your big brother was inside it. Boy was exactly the kind of friend she needed for her secret plan.

Twenty-two

Boy and Audrey sat on the Jenkins's narrow back porch. Busy eating scones, they watched a rain shower sweep the yard. Audrey stuck out her tongue to catch raindrops. The rain didn't last long, but it was enough to make the tin walls of the house glisten.

Douglas was inside, playing with kittens that belonged to Jessie, the sister with the missing tooth.

'Do you get rain up your way?' asked Boy, his mouth full of yellow scone.

'Not too often.' Audrey licked butter from

the corner of her mouth. The scone was delicious, but not quite as light as the ones her mum made.

The door behind them flew open. Douglas stood there with his hands on his hips. 'Audwey, are snails poison?'

'No, I don't think so.'

'Good, cos I kissed one.' The door slammed again, followed by the sound of running feet.

Audrey looked at Boy and remembered Mrs Paterson's remark about runny noses being a bad habit. 'You've got a foydool on your cheek.'

'What?'

Audrey tapped her cheek to show him which side of his face was smeared. Boy wiped his cheek with one sleeve.

'That's a word Mrs Paterson told me.'

Parker bounced a ball off a side wall of the house. Then a scuffed shoe came hurtling out of an open window. A girl climbed out after it.

'Is Mrs P as scary as she looks?' asked Boy.

'I think she's sad.' Audrey said nothing about the crying she had heard late at night. 'But she'll be happier now because I'm her project.'

'What's that mean?'

'I have to say *please* and *thank you* and learn to knit bunny holes.'

'I wouldn't want to be a project if you had to knit.' Boy rolled his eyes. 'Me dad reckons he's seen better heads than Mrs Paterson's on his beer.'

Two of the brothers—Audrey couldn't remember their names—began a mock sword fight with sticks in the backyard.

'Are there lots of children at the school?' asked Audrey.

'About twenty, if everyone turns up.'

'Do you like school?'

'There are *some* good things. Our last teacher had some of those cycle-pedia books. My favourite part was about William the Conqueror. He wore a metal hat that came down over his nose and he got to be King of England.'

'My mum teaches me,' said Audrey. 'But we haven't done conquerers yet.'

'William the Conqueror blew up at his funeral. They tried to make him look like he wasn't dead. But they didn't do it right. You know, like stuffin' a bird.'

'My brother, Price, skins rabbits.' Audrey thought for a moment. 'Was the Conqueror wearing his nose-hat when he exploded?'

'Don't know. That teacher left Beltana and she took her cycle-pedias with her.'

'We're friends now, aren't we?' asked Audrey.

'Reckon so.'

'Would you help me do something?' she said. 'It might get us in trouble.'

Twenty-three

Audrey stood outside the hospital and looked up at the sky. Dark grey clouds promised more rain. Audrey's blue dress was measled with wet dots.

'*Aaah.*' Boy bent over, clutching his stomach. '*Ooh.*'

Audrey frowned.

Boy straightened up. 'I'm just practisin'.'

His rehearsal was so real that it had tricked Audrey for a moment.

'Let's do it now,' she said. 'Me and Dougie have to be back at Mrs Paterson's soon.

Are you really sure it's that window?'

'Yes. I looked through it once. Hughie dared me. They named this new part of the hospital after a lady that died. Her name was Amy Fairfax. The nursing sisters put ladies and babies in there.'

Dragging one leg, Boy limped forward.

'*Psst. Boy*. You're supposed to have a sore stomach. Not a broken leg.'

He nodded but kept the limp.

Audrey began counting.

Boy disappeared around the back of the hospital. Before Audrey even got to a hundred, she heard him give a loud yell.

There were only two nursing sisters in Beltana. If Boy made enough noise, they should both run out to see what was wrong. Audrey crossed her fingers. She heard Boy complaining loudly about pains in his stomach. He was making more racket than a flock of cockatoos.

Audrey sneaked past the rainwater tank and behind some scraggly bushes, heading towards the women's ward. She checked left, and then right, to make sure no one was watching, then peered through the window. There were several beds, but only two had people in them—Audrey's mother and one other woman.

It was polite to knock when you wanted to walk through someone's door. Audrey supposed it was the same for climbing through a window. She rapped on the glass, slid the window open, then hooked one leg over the sill.

Twenty-four

Mum's face was as pale as the sheet that covered her. She sat, propped against pillows in a high iron bed.

Against one wall of the room was a red chair with two big wheels at the front and a small one at the back. Audrey guessed it was for people who couldn't walk.

The other patient was deeply asleep. Her snoring was a dead giveaway. But in a snoring competition, Douglas would still win.

'Fair dinkum,' said Audrey. 'You're a sight for sore eyes, Mum.'

Mum whispered back, 'What are you doing here?'

'I've come to see if you're still alive.' Audrey took her mother's hand.

'I *am*.'

'I know. You're talking.' They smiled at each other.

'The sisters might be cross if they find you here.'

'I washed my hands three times so there's no germs.'

'I'm sure there isn't.' Mum's fingers twitched against Audrey's.

More shouting came from the back of the hospital.

'My goodness. Something's going on out there.'

'My friend, Boy, is distractionating the nurses, so I could sneak in.'

Mum winced. 'He's doing a good job.'

The woman in the next bed didn't move. Her mouth hung open as she snored.

Somewhere at the back of the building, a

baby cried. It reminded Audrey of the way baby birds nagged for attention. 'Can you come home soon, Mum?'

'Soon. When I stop feeling so sick.'

'I don't expect Mrs Paterson is used to people spitting up at her house.'

'Certainly not.'

'That would be on her "Don't" list, for sure.' Audrey saw her letter folded neatly on the bedside table. 'Did you like my letter? It was long and I did it all by myself.'

'It made me smile,' said Mum. 'Are you and Dougie all right?'

'Yes. He said a whole sentence. And I've got a project. I'm looking for Mrs Paterson's good side. You know, like Dad says.'

Her mother's face went pink when Audrey said 'Dad'.

'It's harder than I thought, but I found *some* good things already. Mrs Paterson is knitting me a red thing. It's going to have arms. She likes books. Her hands are soft . . . for an old lady. She let me make her a cup of tea and she only told me what to do five times.'

Mum's eyes looked moist. 'It's lovely to see you, but you'd better go now. I don't want you to get into trouble.'

Reluctantly, Audrey agreed with her mum. Mrs Paterson's 'Don't' list for outside the house didn't include sneaking into the hospital. But only because she hadn't thought of it.

Boy's shouting had stopped. Perhaps he had lost his voice.

Audrey hugged her mother, wishing it would go on forever, but knowing it could not.

Twenty-five

Audrey and Douglas followed Mrs Paterson into the 'Smith of Dunesk' mission church.

Excitement tightened inside Audrey. She tried not to think about the store they were visiting next and what treasures might be there.

First, Mrs Paterson had to do a duty with some flowers. Audrey was glad the goats hadn't eaten them all.

'*Kookookaakaa . . .*' Douglas mimicked his favourite bird at the top of his voice.

Mrs Paterson turned her head to give him

a stern look over the flowers she was carrying. '*Sssh.*'

Douglas's call was loud, but the church was empty. If God made birds in the first place, he wouldn't be upset if someone liked them so much they made bird noises in his house.

'Wait here while I fetch a vase.' Mrs Paterson headed for the back of the church.

The bumpy mission walls were white-washed. Long, wooden benches stretched across bare floorboards. On the far wall was a plastered ribbon. The writing on it said, *Seek ye the Lord while He may be Found.*

Mrs Paterson returned with the flowers in a white vase and sat them on a table. Audrey wished she had thought to take her mum some lavender yesterday. But a hug was better than flowers.

Douglas stuck his thumb in his mouth.

'*Ye* is a funny name, isn't it, Mrs Paterson?' said Audrey. 'Is he from another country? He sounds like a China man.'

Mrs Paterson made a spluttering noise that Audrey couldn't quite work out. It must have been a squashed sneeze caused by flower pollen.

'*Ye* means You,' the old lady said.

'Someone couldn't spell too proper then.'

Mrs Paterson fiddled the lavender to each side of the vase. 'It's Old English. No one speaks that way any more.'

Audrey sat on one of the hard, wooden benches. 'Is that another one of those dead-thing languages?'

'I suppose you could put it that way.' Mrs Paterson bent to scoop up a stray petal that had drifted to the floor.

'So why did someone write dead words on the wall?'

'Oh child! The things you say.' Mrs Paterson's eyebrows rose. 'The *meaning* is not dead. It tells us to look for the Lord.'

Audrey scratched her head while she thought hard about that one. 'But isn't He invisible?'

'You look into your heart ... and in the Good Book. There are ways to find Him.'

A warm feeling swept through Audrey. She glanced out through the open doorway to where Stumpy waited on the path. Mrs Paterson *did* believe in things that were invisible.

Twenty-six

Mrs Paterson, her neck stiff, strode past the Royal Victoria Hotel. She walked faster than usual. 'Riffraff,' she muttered.

The way Mrs Paterson said 'riffraff' made the hotel sound like a bad place. But the verandah was clean and the plants in tubs were neat and green. The schoolteacher lived in the hotel, so it couldn't be too bad. Boy had told Audrey that she gave handers to children who got up to tricks, so she didn't stand any nonsense.

It would hurt a lot to be whacked on the

hand with a cane. The teacher had already given Boy handers eight times. Audrey was impressed. Even though she didn't think it was too smart to put flies in the teacher's drinking water.

Boy also said that there was a table in the front room of the hotel where people hit balls with sticks and tried to get them into little holes. That would be fun. But a visit to the store would be better than a peek in a hotel. The store had lollies.

'We *must* get you a pair of decent shoes, my girl,' said Mrs Paterson. 'Those boots belong in the bush.'

'That's a true thing,' said Audrey, 'I *live* in the bush, Mrs Paterson.'

'*That* is obvious.'

Douglas didn't care about shoes. He didn't bother to wear them most of the time. At home, he only went for shoes when the three-cornered jack prickles were bad.

Audrey and Douglas followed Mrs Paterson into the store.

Goods of all kinds were stacked from the floor almost to the ceiling. There were more things in one room than in the whole of Audrey's house.

'Do not touch unless you intend to buy,' said Mrs Paterson.

Douglas's little fingers went straight to the handlebars of a bicycle. He tilted his head to look at it sideways. Audrey wondered how people could ride bicycles without falling off. But then, people balanced on horses without falling too often. Gently, she guided her brother away from the bicycles and pedal cars.

The store shelves were loaded with packets, jars, tins and bottles. Audrey saw colourful biscuit tins, Vincent's Powders for headaches, Fowler's Lion Brand herbs and Life Savers, lollies with a hole in the middle. Maybe you could stick your tongue in it for fun. Boy's sister, Jessie, might like them.

Every time Douglas saw something he liked, he tugged at Audrey's hand. She hoped he wouldn't pull free and run off. He'd be sure to knock something over.

Two women stood at the high front counter, chatting. They said hello to Mrs Paterson, then kept talking without pausing for breath. One of the women wore lipstick so red it looked like the setting sun after a bushfire. She asked her friend, 'Did you hear about the Jenkins boy?'

Pins and needles ran down Audrey's arms.

'He had a sudden attack of appendicitis. Stopped as quickly as it started. He was lucky.'

'Quite a fuss at the hospital. He made enough noise to wake the dead.' The woman pushed at the corner of her lips with one finger, as though she was worried her lipstick was sliding away.

'No good ever came of listening to gossip,' said Mrs Paterson from behind Audrey.

Audrey jumped.

She wanted to hear what the woman said about Boy. It had been her plan that sent him to the hospital, clutching his stomach and wailing. Audrey didn't like keeping the secret, but Mrs Paterson would be as cross as two sticks if she found out.

The gossiping women moved onto another topic.

Douglas stood with his face glued to the counter that had the lollies. Audrey spied some ribbons. Brightly coloured and in small rolls, they looked like a rainbow that had been separated into strips.

Mrs Paterson moved to stand beside Audrey. Her black dress rustled. The smell of lavender hung about her.

'Leaping lizards!' said Audrey. 'Aren't they pretty?'

'I cannot imagine what lizards have to do with ribbons.'

Audrey thought about tying yellow ribbons onto the end of her thick, fair plaits.

'You'd look nice with that one.' Audrey

pointed to a roll of thin ribbon that was the blue of a summer sky.

Mrs Paterson stiffened. 'I only wear black.' Her voice was tight. Twin patches of pink appeared high on her cheeks.

Sometimes what people *didn't* say was more curious that what they *did* say. Audrey wondered if she was the only one keeping a secret.

'May I please try on the black ones?'

Twenty-seven

Audrey stared at a pair of shiny black shoes. Her mouth started to water. She used to think that only happened if you were hungry and saw food. Now she knew shoes made it happen too.

She swallowed, and then reached out to stroke one of the black shoes. It had a large bow on top and a thick heel. She screwed up her face, then grinned.

'Whatever are you doing, Audrey Barlow?'

Audrey looked up.

Mrs Paterson had a pair of brown lace-ups in her hand. Solid and squat, they looked dull compared to the shiny black pair.

'I can see my face in the shiny stuff.'

'Sit there.' Mrs Paterson pointed to a stool. 'Try this brown pair on.'

Audrey felt disappointment like a lead weight in her chest. She dragged herself over to the stool and plonked herself onto it. Then she slowly slid off her old boots and wriggled her bare toes.

Douglas danced over to watch.

Mrs Paterson held out a brown shoe. Audrey put it on. It felt stiff, heavy and uncomfortable.

'Try both on and take a few steps to see how they feel.' Mrs Paterson looked over the top of her small round glasses.

Audrey plodded up and down.

'You look like a cow,' said Douglas. 'You got big feet.'

Audrey giggled.

Mrs Paterson sighed.

'May I please try on the black ones?' asked Audrey. Her voice was calm but her heart was going pitter-pat.

Mrs Paterson sighed again. Audrey took that as a *yes*. She removed the brown lace-ups and put on the black shoes.

'Bet I don't look like a cow with these on, do I, Dougie?' Audrey whispered.

'No.' Douglas jiggled on his little legs. 'You look like an *emu*. I want lollies now. Owinge ones.'

Her chin raised, Audrey walked just the way Mrs Paterson had done past the hotel.

'Why are you walking in that ridiculous manner? Are the shoes too tight?'

Audrey shook her head. 'This is how *you* walk, Mrs Paterson.'

The old lady's eyebrows shot up. 'Nonsense. If I held my nose that high in the air I could not see where I was placing my feet.'

Mrs Paterson hadn't seen herself walking, so she probably didn't know how she did it.

'I could be a lady in these black shoes,' said Audrey in her sweetest voice. The one that always made her dad suspicious.

'I suppose it wouldn't hurt. They fit. And they do look as though they might last, *if* you treat them carefully.'

'I'll really look after them. I'll spit on 'em and everything.'

'I beg your pardon?'

'Dad says that you have to spit on your shoes to make them really shiny. He calls it *spit and polish*. Not that he cleans *his* boots. They're too old, but ...' Audrey faltered. 'Course, he's a man and men are allowed to spit. We don't, because we're ladies, aren't we?'

'I hardly think spitting of *any* sort should be encouraged.'

'Too right.' Audrey nodded.

Mrs Patterson pursed her lips, then said, 'I suppose if a simple pair of black shoes prompted an improvement in your manners, that would be a good thing.'

'Fair dinkum.' Audrey slapped her thigh with one hand. 'I'll look like the cocky's corsets.'

Twenty-eight

Audrey and Boy sat on a large rock, just outside of town. The rain had cleared, but there were still puddles on the ground. Audrey wished there was a way to take the puddles back home to the bush.

'It's better watchin' the trains out here than at the station,' said Boy. 'We got it all to ourselves.'

'Is it time yet?' Audrey leant forward for a better look along the railway line.

'Sometimes it's late if sand has blown on the track. Dad says they sometimes hand out shovels to the passengers so they can help clear it. Me dad's a guard. He's got a hat and everything.'

'Will the train have lots of carriages?'

'Depends how many passengers there are. And today's newspaper day. The papers come three times a week.' Boy sniffed. 'I got long trousers.'

'Me too, 'cept mine fall down because they were my brother's. I have to wear braces.'

'Mine are too short at the ankles because I grew so much lately. But there aren't any patches or rips. The knees are shiny, but knees don't matter much.'

'I reckon braces are more important than knees. Do you?'

'Too right.' Boy cleared his throat. 'I don't have a fancy tie like Dad. But I look all right in me trousers.' His tone hinted that he was working up to something important. But when Audrey looked at him, he glanced away.

'I wear long trousers to dances,' he said. 'Can you dance?'

'Sort of. It's more like jumping. Before the dances start, we get wax flakes from old candles and sweep them onto the floor of the hall. Then we jump on sandbags and slip all round the place to shine it up. Someone falls over every year. It's real funny.'

Audrey wondered what it would be like whirling round and round on that dance floor. 'I've never been to a dance,' she said.

'There's cakes for supper. Mrs Dawson makes apple cider with more bang than a dunny door. That's what Dad say, anyways. There's a dance this Saturday night. I can hescort you if you want.'

'What's *hescort*?'

'When you let a girl hang on your arm so she doesn't fall over in her good clothes. I seen Dad do it for Mum.'

Audrey felt a tug of longing. 'I don't

know if Mrs Paterson would let me go. She might not like dancing.'

'Well, she used to. Dad said her foxtrot looked so real he thought she might grow a tail and start chasin' chooks. Mrs P and her husband were the only ones who knowed how to do that foxtrot. They learnt it from an American man. But she stopped when Mr Paterson and then her son, Lionel, died. Guess there was no one she wanted to dance with after that.'

Audrey couldn't picture the old lady dancing, even when she closed her eyes and tried especially hard. Perhaps Mrs Paterson was sad because her feet wanted to dance, but her head wouldn't let them.

'I can get Mum to ask Mrs P if you can go,' suggested Boy.

The *choof, choof, choof* of a steam engine announced the train was around the bend.

Audrey leapt to her feet. 'There it is!'

Smoke puffed up above the trees. Then

the black engine showed its nose. The wheels squealed along the tracks.

Behind the driver's cabin was a tender loaded with coal.

'A fireman shovels that coal,' said Boy. 'I might do that when I get older. I'm strong cos I eat porridge every morning.'

The maroon-coloured carriages rattled along behind the engine. The couplings connecting them clanged and banged.

Audrey waved as though she was trying to shake her arm loose. The driver waved back. But it was a more gentle wave. One that wouldn't damage his steering arm. Then he pulled the rope that blew the whistle.

Some of the passengers waved too.

'The engine breathes smoke like a dragon,' said Audrey.

They watched till the train vanished around the next bend. And then they kept watching as the smoke went too.

Audrey sighed with satisfaction, then said, 'Yes.'

'Yes what?'

'If Mrs Paterson lets me, I'll come to the dance. I've never been hescorted.'

'Good-o.' Boy stood up and dusted his hands on the back of his shorts. 'Come on, there's somethin' else I want to show you.'

Audrey jumped to her feet. She knew all the best places back home—her cubbyhouses, the scrubby patch where the daddy emus walked with their striped babies, the giant ant hills, the sandy slope that was good fun to slide down on sheets of tin. But here, everything was unfamiliar. 'Where are we going?'

'Me favourite place.'

Twenty-nine

Audrey turned in a circle. 'Is *this* your favourite place?'

A rabbit dashed out of a hole in the ground, hopped across the dry grass, and then vanished behind a headstone.

'We're takin' a shortcut. It's over there.' Boy pointed to the trees that Audrey had seen when her family first trundled into town in the cart. 'But I catch lots of rabbits here in the graveyard. I used to sell more of 'em but people found out where I was catchin' 'em.'

Audrey would have lots to tell her family when they were back together. Her chest tightened as she thought of home. She remembered the crooked kitchen table, the aroma of fresh scones and Mum in her apron, her cheeks pink from cooking. Audrey imagined Dad in the kitchen too, sneaking scones while they were still hot. And Douglas, jumping up to touch the dried fruit that hung from the kitchen ceiling. Then Audrey thought about Price ruffling his messy hair, which usually made it look even more untidy.

If Mrs Paterson was right about the *expecting*, there would be another little Barlow to fit into the tiny kitchen at home. Audrey hoped it would be a girl. Brothers were all right. But a girl would be better.

Stumpy pulled a face. Audrey knew he was trying to make her giggle.

She rolled her eyes. 'You were supposed to stay at the Jenkins's house with Dougie.'

'Who are you talkin' to?' asked Boy.

Audrey hesitated. Mrs Paterson's face had gone prune-shaped when she heard about Stumpy. But Boy didn't seem fussy. And now Audrey and Boy were friends. 'Stumpy. He's my camel. He's mostly invisible. You can only see him if you believe he's there.'

Boy stared as though he was looking at Stumpy. But he was facing the wrong way. 'Do you call him Stumpy because he's short?'

'No. When I first told my dad about him, he said, "Cut me off at the knees and call me Stumpy". So I thought that was a good name.'

'I used to play with a pirate when I was little. And no one could see *him*.'

'Beltana is a long way from the sea,' said Audrey. She had played pirates too. But she *was* the pirate. She hadn't *seen* one.

'He was shipwrecked,' said Boy. 'So he crawled up the beach and got on a train. The train stopped here.'

That made sense. Except that a pirate was

made up. Stumpy was real. But she didn't want to tell Boy that. He might feel hurt.

Boy tapped a headstone. 'I knowed some of these people. I come out and talk to 'em sometimes.'

Audrey nodded. 'I talk to my sisters, Pearl and Esther. They're out the back of our house.'

'There's stories in here, if you can read proper.'

The stone beside Audrey named Anne Johnson and her four children, who died in a fire.

'Are there ghosts here?' asked Audrey.

'They don't come out in the daytime.'

'Do you think people mostly see ghosts at night because they're white?'

'Maybe.' Boy started walking towards the trees.

Audrey beckoned Stumpy to follow, even though a few minutes earlier she had scolded him for following her. She felt safer with him close by. Careful not to step on any of the mounds of earth, she headed after Boy.

'A swaggie called Toothless told me that a headless ghost rides past the graves at Kanyaka at midnight,' said Audrey.

'Knock me bandy!'

'It'd be hard doing hauntings if you couldn't see. You'd bang into things. Doors, walls, horses. Even other ghosts.' A fly landed on Audrey's right cheek and she swished it away.

Boy scrambled down an embankment, with Audrey right behind him. At the bottom was a creek. Audrey skidded on small rocks, wobbled, then regained her balance. She was glad she was wearing her old boots, not her new black shoes. 'Do you reckon ladies climb down to look at creeks?'

'Ladies can do whatever they like. Except, maybe, burp at the table. Even me mum don't let anyone do that.'

Boy sat back on his heels at the edge of the creek and lifted a rock from the water. Tadpoles swam in all directions.

'My dad ate tadpoles once,' said Audrey. 'An Aboriginal man fried them for him. The good part was they were crunchy. Bad part was they were really small. He said you'd have to eat a whole creek of 'em to fill you up.'

Boy wrinkled his nose. His stomach didn't like what his ears were hearing.

'My dad says we ain't never allowed to camp near a creek.' Boy shooed a fly off his lip. 'A flash flood can come up while you're asleep. And you wouldn't know nothin' about it because there could be a big storm on the other side of the ranges that you couldn't see. A flash flood can wash you away and, when you wake up, you're dead.'

'Too right?'

Boy nodded.

'Where do you reckon ghosts keep their heads?'

Dear Mum,

My new frend, Boy, arsked to hescort me to a dance on Saturday. He will wear his long trousers with the shiny ~~nees~~ knees.

Every time they have a dance someone comes a cropper so there is always something to larf about. There will be a man playing the squeeze box, so we don't have to hum our own music. There will be lots of food. ~~Enugh~~ Enough to make people feel sick. Which is good.

Boy says his dad can cut the eye out of a mozzie with his stock whip. I havnt met his dad yet. When he comes back home, I hope there are some mozzies so I can see if its true.

Mrs Paterson has shoes that lace all the way to her ankools, so they hold up her legs. She bought me a new pair of shoes. They look pretty. Not like hers.

I hope Mrs Paterson lets me go to the dance. If you arnt too sick can you arsk her? <u>Please.</u>

Stumpy runs away a lot here. I call him but he won't answer.

Hope you feel better soon so we can go home. (But I want to show you the ribbins in the store first.)

Love from your Audrey, Dougie and Stumpy

P.S. Do you know what a <u>riff raff</u> is?

Thirty

Mrs Paterson sat in Mrs Jenkins's house with her hands folded. Her gloves looked out of place in the untidy kitchen. It was full of dishes and tins that Mrs Jenkins hadn't had time to put away. With ten children she probably *never* had time. When number ten finished eating, number one would be hungry again. Audrey hated to think how many dishes there would be to wash and dry.

Audrey straightened her back to sit like the old lady. But she couldn't manage it quite so perfectly.

'I'm not sure it's proper,' said Mrs Paterson in a loud voice.

Audrey scarcely dared to breathe, in case it brought the word *No* from Mrs Paterson's lips.

Stumpy stared in through the kitchen window. He didn't mind rain. His thick eyelashes kept water out of his eyes.

Some of the Jenkins boys were shouting at the other end of the house. Audrey wasn't sure which ones. Then came thumping. But nothing flew out of the window this time. They must have been playing, not fighting.

Douglas picked up an orange kitten by the scruff of the neck. 'He wants to come wiv me.'

Jessie giggled and poked the tip of her tongue through her teeth. She would miss that gap when her tooth came down.

'He's only little, Dougie,' said Audrey. 'He needs his mummy.'

Douglas's face went pink and his eyes

were sad. He was thinking about their own mum, Audrey could tell. She wished she hadn't said the word. But it was too late to take it back.

Jessie grabbed the kitten from Douglas and headed into another room. Douglas scooted after her. Soon there was the sound of giggling, followed by the *meow* of a cat.

'A dance might be just the thing to take small minds off large matters.' Mrs Jenkins lifted the end of her green apron and dabbed at the perspiration on her face. 'It'll use up some of that excess energy children have.'

'The railwaymen will come into town.'

'My Bert is a railwayman,' said Mrs Jenkins. 'He'll be home on the weekend. He won't let any of them get up to too much nonsense.'

Mrs Jenkins herself could make anybody behave. She was used to bossing all the people in her family.

'Boy will look after Audrey. And I'll take

the little 'un under my wing.' Mrs Jenkins made herself sound like a chook. But then, her brood of children *were* like chickens around a hen.

Finally, Mrs Paterson nodded. 'I'll think about it.'

Audrey smiled. There was a chance that she would get to the dance.

The old lady stood up, buttoning her overcoat. 'Rain or no rain, we must go. It's only water, after all.' She stepped outside to pop open her large black umbrella.

Audrey and Douglas didn't mind rain. On the way home Douglas stomped into the first puddle he saw. And kept jumping in every puddle after that. At first, Mrs Paterson tried to stop him. But he ignored her. So she just kept a safe distance from the splashes.

Although Audrey was wearing her old boots and she liked to splash too, she didn't join in. If she could last the next few days without doing anything wrong, the old lady might trust her enough to let her go to the dance.

Stumpy clomped along behind them. Mrs Paterson didn't know that, and Audrey didn't tell her.

Blinking water from her eyes, Audrey grabbed the old lady's hand and squeezed. 'Mrs Paterson, are raindrops different shapes?'

Mrs Paterson didn't squeeze back, but neither did she withdraw her hand or scold. 'It is not a question to which I have devoted much thought.'

'If you let me go to the dance Saturday night I'll be good,' promised Audrey. 'I'll only *dance* with Boy. I won't marry him.'

'*Marry* him?' repeated Mrs Paterson.

'I have to grow up first. Boy's my friend. But we don't marry men with foydools, do we?'

Audrey tipped the left-over dishwater on the garden.

Thirty-one

Audrey felt the warm sun through the fabric of her smock. The previous day's clouds had moved away. The sky was blue and clear. Careful not to spill water on her boots, Audrey tipped the left-over dishwater on the garden. Just as Mrs Paterson had instructed.

The old lady adjusted her straw hat, then continued trimming the leaves of a grey bush with a large pair of scissors. Douglas sat on the ground, pushing a stick through the damp dirt and making *vroom, vroom* noises. Now that he'd seen a car, he imagined one in every piece of wood or stone.

'That grey bush smells funny,' said Audrey.

'It's wormwood. Grows anywhere and it's as tough as old boots.'

Audrey tipped the last drops of water from the tin bowl. 'Mrs Paterson, can I ...' She corrected herself. '*May* I ask you something?'

Mrs Paterson looked doubtful, but she said, 'If it is not too personal.'

Audrey swung the bowl in one hand. Drips flew sideways. 'How do I know if it's too personal?'

'I suppose I'll have to tell you, won't I?'

'But I'd have to ask it first. Then, if you said it was too personal, it would be too late. I would already have asked it.'

'Must you always make everything so complicated?' said Mrs Paterson. 'Is it about religion, money or politics?'

'I don't *think* so.'

'*Vroom, vroom,*' said Douglas. His stick-car turned a wide circle in the mud.

'Speak then,' Mrs Paterson told Audrey.

'Why don't you like colours?'

The old lady paused for a moment, then she said, 'I am in mourning.'

'But it's the afternoon.'

'I mean that I am remembering someone who died ... This is hardly the place to discuss such things.'

'I'm good at keeping secrets.'

'It is no *secret*. The whole town knows.'

'Would you tell *me* then?'

Mrs Paterson mouth tightened as though she was not going to answer. Then she said. 'My son, Lionel.'

'Is he one of the men in the photos on your mantelpiece?' said Audrey. 'Was he sick?'

'You ask too many questions. Children should be seen and not heard.'

'But then we wouldn't find out anything.'

Mrs Paterson sighed. 'He was killed in the Great War. In 1917.'

'That's a long time with no colour.'

Mrs Paterson's face looked like a crumpled cloth.

'My two sisters, Pearl and Esther, died when they were little,' said Audrey. 'But I don't reckon they'd want me to be sad for a long time. They'd want me to have colours. What's your son's favourite colour?'

'I am not certain. Perhaps . . . blue.'

'You'd look pretty in blue. It's the colour of your eyes,' said Audrey. 'I don't want *my* mum to be sad. I bet Lionel wouldn't want you to be either.'

The old lady was quiet. Perhaps she was remembering her Lionel.

'I'm a girl so I can't be a son,' said Audrey, determined to cheer the old lady up. 'But I'm your project. That's the next best thing.'

Thirty-two

Audrey sat on a stool at Mrs Paterson's feet in the sitting room. Despite the metal screen with its pattern of Afghans and camels, the fire heated Audrey's back. She held Mrs Paterson's fingers, massaging hand cream into her skin. The afternoon's gardening had left a few scratches, but nothing deep or painful.

The old lady's eyes were half-closed. Although her cheeks were unusually red, she made no move to shift away from the fire.

Douglas rolled across the floor, from one

wall to the other. Then he stopped and sat up. 'Howolderyu?'

'What did that boy say?' Mrs Paterson spoke without fully opening her eyes.

'How old are you?' repeated Audrey, smoothing a trail of hand cream over Mrs Paterson's knuckles.

The old lady's eyes did shoot open then. 'Young man, it is rude to ask a lady how old she is.'

Douglas poked one finger in his ear. 'I got blue undies.'

'Well, really.'

The red dots on Mrs Paterson's cheeks spread across her face. 'Underclothing is not a suitable topic for conversation in a sitting room.'

Audrey suspected Mrs Paterson would not discuss undies in *any* room.

'Thank you. That will do nicely.' Mrs Patterson withdrew her hand from Audrey's. 'I suggest we put our minds to a higher place.'

'Heaven?' guessed Audrey.

'Not quite that high.' Mrs Paterson's mouth twitched in an almost-smile. 'Perhaps you would like to write your mother another letter. She will be missing you.'

'That's the *best* idea in the whole *world*.'

'Thank you for the praise, but I feel it's a trifle overdone.' Despite her protest, Mrs Paterson looked pleased.

'What will I tell her about the dance?' Audrey watched the old lady's face for any sign of a 'yes' or 'no'.

Douglas rolled back across the room and thumped against the far wall. Audrey waited for him to cry, but he didn't. He seemed to like thumping as much as he liked rolling. Douglas rolled again and came to a stop at Mrs Paterson's feet, 'What age were you when you were my age?'

She looked down at him with one raised eyebrow.

'If I went to the dance, I'd wear my yellow dress,' said Audrey. 'It's only got one mend in it and you can't really see it. Boy's got long trousers. But girls don't wear trousers to dances. They don't twizzle.'

Mrs Paterson put one hand to her forehead. 'I beg your pardon?'

'*Twizzle*. It's one of my special words. I made it up. You twizzle like this.' Audrey got up and spun round. The hem of her blue dress floated up around her.

'You are making me dizzy.'

'I reckon *you'd* be a really good twizzler,' said Audrey.

The old lady looked up at the photos on the mantelpiece. 'Perhaps I was. Once.' Light from the fire shone on her face. She looked happier when her skin was bright.

'Boy's dad said you dance like a fox.'

Beltana, April 1930

Dear Mum

I am being VERY good and nemembering please and
Thank you.

When Stumpy is here I make him stay quiet.
He plays with his new friends from the camel farm
when I go to the Jenkins house.

I am writing a new list so you can see the Do
things—

<u>Brush your hair 100 times every night</u> (but then you
lie on your hair and mess it up).

<u>Don't turn your fork over the other way when you
eat peas</u> (this is silly ~~becos~~ because the peas fall
off—unless you stab them, but then they roll off
the plate).

<u>When you finish your food, push the ~~nife~~ knife
and fork together so people know you are finished</u>
(you could just tell them but I think Mrs Paterson likes
to work it out for herself).

<u>Say Thank you for everything you can think of
before you eat</u> (so your food tastes ~~betta~~ better. But
arsking for a blessing for the poor is like arsking for
something for yourself if you are one of them so if
you are poor you should bless the rich so you aren't
arsking for something for yourself.)

<u>On washing day hang your undies where no one
can see them</u> or they will know you wear them.

Love from your Audrey, Dougie and Stumpy

Thirty-three

Audrey wrenched open the front door and ran down the hallway, through the dining room, kitchen and into the laundry. 'Mrs Paterson!'

Douglas belted along behind her, making noises that not even Audrey could interpret.

The old lady turned her head. Her sleeves were rolled up and her hands were submerged in water in the laundry trough. 'What has happened?'

'Mum's coming home on Monday and she's stopped spitting up ... I mean, she's *feeling better.'* Audrey waved a sheet of paper. 'Boy came over with this. Mrs Jenkins sent him. It's a note from Mum.'

'I am happy that you will have your mother back,' said Mrs Paterson.

Douglas, his face pink with delight, bounced over and grabbed her leg.

'Dougie, don't squeeze Mrs Paterson's arthritis,' said Audrey.

'Perhaps if he adjusts his grip, I will not lose my leg.' Mrs Paterson's voice was steady, but Audrey thought she heard a laugh at the back of it.

Douglas didn't budge.

Mrs Paterson lifted the clothing she was washing out of the water.

'Is that my yellow dress?' asked Audrey, suddenly breathless.

'I believe so.'

'Am I going to the dance tomorrow?'

'If you wish . . .'

'I do. I *wish.'* Audrey clapped her hands. 'This is my best day ever. I can go to the dance *and* Mum's coming back.'

Mrs Paterson began squeezing the water from the yellow dress. 'It would reflect badly on this household if you were not permitted to attend.'

'Can me and Boy be your hescort?'

'*Escort*. There is no such word as *hescort*. Where do you get these expressions from?'

'It's my dead language,' said Audrey, 'like "ye" and the numbers on the clock.'

'I wanna dance too,' yelled Douglas. His voice bounced off the laundry walls.

Mrs Paterson shook her head. 'It is not polite to shout, young man. Speak quietly.'

'Quoitly,' shouted Douglas.

'When your dress is dry, Audrey, I will press it. Just because you are poor, doesn't mean you have to be unkempt.'

'I'm not poor. I've got my family.'

The old lady's mouth tightened.

'You're coming to the dance too, aren't you?'

Mrs Paterson did not answer.

Thirty-four

Audrey stared at herself in Mrs Paterson's long mirror. Turning left and right, she couldn't see one crease in the yellow dress. Her face was pink with excitement and her green eyes, clear and bright. Audrey's hair gleamed after its hundred brushstrokes. She wished her mum could see her shiny hair and new shoes. When Mum came out of hospital there would be so much to tell her.

'I put a touch of starch in the water, to stiffen the material of your dress. It looks almost new,' said Mrs Paterson.

Douglas stared at Audrey, his thumb in his mouth. 'You look priddy.'

'Thank you, Dougie.' Audrey leaned over to kiss his cheek.

Douglas pulled away and made a face. 'Yuck.'

'He will grow out of it,' said Mrs Paterson. 'They always do.'

'I know he will,' said Audrey. 'He kisses snails.'

Mrs Paterson stared down at Douglas as though she was imagining the snail and didn't like it.

Audrey swished from side to side. 'Will I crackle like you?'

'What do you mean?'

'Your dress crackles when you walk.'

'Perhaps it is my arthritic knees.'

'Cake,' said Douglas.

'Yes, there'll be cake,' Audrey assured him.

'I will give you an old jacket of mine to wear.' As Mrs Paterson tied yellow ribbons at the end of Audrey's plaits, her hands trembled.

'But won't you want to wear it?' asked Audrey.

Mrs Paterson shook her head. 'No one will care in the least whether I am there or not. You and your brother will be safe with the Jenkins family. They may not bathe as often as I would wish, but they are good at heart.'

'If you come you can watch me and Dougie. You can eat the cakes. And you can make sure that Boy doesn't stamp on my feet. I think he could be a real stamper, don't you?'

Mrs Paterson said nothing.

'And I've got a surprise,' added Audrey. 'Boy sold two rabbits to a man who didn't know they came from the graveyard. Anyway, Boy split the money with me because I showed him how Price skins his rabbits and it was better than the way Boy does it. He was starting at the wrong end.'

She slipped one hand into her pocket and pulled out a length of narrow ribbon the colour of a summer sky. 'I bought you this.'

The old lady stared.

Audrey hoped she wasn't angry.

But Mrs Paterson took the ribbon. She ran one finger down its length, just the way Audrey had done in the store.

'We'll both look pretty,' said Audrey.

'Pretty *wrinkled*, in my case. The ribbon is lovely. Just the thing to wear around my neck. Thank you.'

A loud knock at the door announced that Boy and some of his brothers or sisters had arrived. Douglas ran out into the hallway.

'Please say you'll come to the dance, Mrs Paterson.'

'I am not dressed properly.' Mrs Paterson looked down at Audrey. 'But it would be a pity to waste such a beautiful ribbon. You go ahead. I will meet you there.'

'Promise?'

'I promise.'

'Remember,' said Audrey, with one finger raised, 'Ladies don't tell fibs. Not if they might get caught, anyways.'

'I'm hescorting you.'

Thirty-five

The wind was nippy. Audrey was glad that Mrs Paterson had loaned her the jacket. Audrey carried her new black shoes in one hand. Her old boots would do for the walk to the hall.

Boy took her elbow. 'I'm not gunna push you over or nothin',' he said. 'I'm hescorting you.'

Audrey didn't tell him the word had no 'h'.

Hugh piggy-backed Douglas. Together, they looked like a giant turtle. Audrey hoped Douglas wasn't squeezing Hugh's neck too tightly.

It was almost dark, but it was only a short walk to the hall.

Moths fluttered around the outside light above the hall door. More light streamed out of the windows. Audrey heard music and voices.

Boy opened the door to the hall. Inside were swirling dresses and long trousers. Feet clomped, slid and tripped. The air was warm, moist and smelled of wax.

Hugh swung Douglas down. The moment Douglas's feet touched the floor, he was off like a racing tadpole. He disappeared among the dancers.

'I'll f . . . f . . . find him,' said Hugh. 'He's p . . . probably looking for Jessie.'

'Or cake,' said Audrey.

She took off her borrowed jacket and swapped her old boots for the new shoes. Boy stood on tiptoes to hang the jacket and Audrey's boots from a big hook on the wall.

Audrey decided not to try dancing just yet. Someone might scuff the perfect shine on her black shoes.

Packed with dancing couples, the hall was decorated with ribbons and the floor gleamed with polish. Audrey heard boots sliding across the floor. The man playing the squeezebox was huge. His legs oozed over the side of the chair.

Boy looked taller in his long trousers. His shirt had no rips and it was clean. But he still had that familiar cheeky gleam in his brown eyes.

The squeezebox player was really putting on a performance, leaning left, then right. His fingers pressed the keys so fast that Audrey could hardly keep track. Underfoot, the wooden floor vibrated as men pushed their partners around like bouncing wheelbarrows.

Mrs Jenkins walked past with Douglas hanging on one arm and Jessie on the other.

'There's me dad.' Boy pointed to a man with fluffy side whiskers. 'Mum says he looks like a ferret.' He gave a lopsided grin. 'Lucky she doesn't mind ferrets.'

Mr Jenkins looked a lot like his boys. Except that he was hairier. Mr Jenkins was thin. Audrey was sure that when he stood next to his plump wife, he would seem even thinner.

The hall door opened. A gust of cold wind blew in.

Audrey turned, expecting Mrs Paterson.

But it was Sylvia. The woman with the fluttering, bird-like hands who had helped on the day Mum had fainted. A tall, bald man walked behind her, close enough to be a breathing shadow.

More people arrived and a few red-faced dancers staggered outside for fresh air.

Audrey felt worry niggling at her. Maybe they should have waited for Mrs Paterson. She was old and her ankle shoes might slow her down.

'Boy.' She tapped his arm. 'Mrs Paterson isn't here yet.'

'Maybe she isn't comin'.'

'She promised. And she was going to wear the blue ribbon around her neck.'

The squeezebox man stopped playing, took out a grey-and-white handkerchief from his pocket and mopped his glistening forehead. Dancers stumbled to a stop, laughing and perspiring.

Suddenly there was a deep rumble from outside, followed by crashing. It sounded like thunder.

People stopped talking. Audrey didn't know what the sound was, but she knew it was bad by the worried expression on everyone's faces. A shiver ran down her spine.

Thirty-six

The bald man who had arrived with Sylvia shot out the door into the darkness.

'What is it?' cried Audrey.

Before Boy could answer, the moving crowd separated them.

Confused, Audrey looked around. 'Dougie!' she called, hoping he would hear and answer.

Mrs Jenkins pushed through to Audrey. She had Douglas on her hip. Both of his arms were tightly around her neck. 'I've got Dougie, Audrey.'

'What is it? What's that noise?'

'Sounds like a flash flood. We had one here a few years back.'

Audrey's heart thumped. She remembered what Boy said about flash floods, and how you could wake up dead.

Mrs Paterson had to walk past the creek to get to the hall.

'Mrs Paterson might be stuck out there!'

A hand grasped her arm. She spun round to see Mr Jenkins. Up close, his side whiskers looked even fluffier. His brown eyes bulged a little. He held a kerosene lantern in his other hand. 'Steady on, little miss.' Several men and a wiry woman gathered behind him. 'I'm sure she's fine, but we'll go and look for her together.'

The cold night air hit Audrey like a wall as she hurried outside. Lanterns bobbed as people strode towards the creek. With the lanterns and the half-moon, it wasn't completely dark. But Audrey still had to be careful not to trip on the uneven ground.

The nearby creek had risen over the path. It gushed, bucked and roared like a wild animal. Branches were pushed along like strips of paper. Something large, with fur, tumbled over and over, and was washed away. Perhaps it was a kangaroo.

Audrey had never seen so much water.

'Careful now, folks,' said Mr Jenkins.

'What's that?' shouted Audrey. 'Over there.'

It was a strip of light blue around Mrs Paterson's neck showing against the midnight black of her dress. She clung to a tree trunk and the water was up to her waist. As Audrey watched, the tree bent, then swayed, with the force of the water. If its roots were dislodged, Mrs Paterson would be swept away with the tree.

Thirty-seven

Mrs Paterson's mouth opened and closed. But the din of the rushing water tore away her words. A tree branch swept passed her. Audrey felt sick at the thought of what would happen if a branch like that hit the old lady.

Mr Jenkins slipped off his jacket and tossed it aside.

Someone handed him a length of rope.

Audrey thought he was going to throw it to Mrs Paterson. But if her hands were frozen, she wouldn't be able to grab hold of it. And if she let go of the tree trunk to take the rope, she might be captured by the angry floodwaters.

Mr Jenkins kicked off his elastic-sided boots, tied the rope around his own waist and waded into the water. The waiting men held firmly to the rope, ready to reel Mr Jenkins—and Mrs Paterson—back to them.

Mr Jenkins edged closer to Mrs Paterson. The rope went slack, then tight, in turns.

He slipped and fell back into the dark water.

Boy shouted something Audrey couldn't quite work out. But she didn't need to hear the actual words to understand that Boy was afraid for his dad.

Mr Jenkins scrambled awkwardly to his feet.

He struggled to get nearer to Mrs Paterson.

Finally, propping himself against the tree trunk, he slipped the rope over his head and looped it about the old lady's waist. Then he flung one arm around her.

People pulled on the rope. Audrey grabbed hold too. Her hands slipped and stung. Boy was beside her, pulling with all his might.

The wobbly tree trunk that Mrs Paterson had clung to snapped and was swept away in the torrent.

Boy's dad and Mrs Paterson came closer to the edge of the creek. Hands reached from the crowd and helped them out.

Audrey let go of the rope, stumbled to Mrs Paterson and hugged her.

'Are you all right?' shouted Audrey. She could feel the old lady shaking.

'I . . . will be. If you loosen your . . . grip. You are . . . squeezing me to death.'

'I do believe that you rescued me.'

Thirty-eight

Audrey sat on a straight-backed chair near Mrs Paterson.

The old woman leant back on the sitting room sofa, a brown knitted rug over her legs. There was a long scratch on her right cheek. A dark bruise was forming under one eye. Her ankle was swollen. As usual, Mrs Paterson's grey hair was pulled into a bun, but two small curls dangled over her forehead.

Douglas lay on the rug in front of the fire, sound asleep, with his thumb jammed in his mouth. His sandy-coloured fringe was damp with perspiration. He had refused to leave either Audrey or Mrs Paterson. But it was late and he had fallen asleep. He twitched, his mind busy with dreams.

Now that everyone had gone back to their own homes, it was quiet except for the crackle of wood in the fire. There was a faint smell of smoke. One of the logs had been a little green.

'Are you sure you don't want to go to the hospital?' Audrey asked Mrs Paterson. 'You could be next to Mum. Until tomorrow when they let her out, anyways.'

'I do *not* need a hospital.' Mrs Paterson's voice reminded Audrey of a bee sting. 'I prefer my own home. Besides, I'm only resting so *you* don't fuss.'

Audrey nodded. 'Resting is on my "Do" list.'

Mrs Paterson raised one eyebrow.

Audrey wasn't afraid of that eyebrow any more. It popped up and down all the time.

'Speaking of the hospital, how are your hands, child?'

Audrey looked down at her red palms. 'They don't hurt.'

'Yes they do. You have rope burn.'

'Maybe a bit.'

'You are as bad as I am,' said Mrs Paterson.

'Fair dinkum.' Audrey let her red hands rest in her lap. 'I'm sorry my new shoes got all scratched.'

'There will be more shoes.' Mrs Paterson tapped her fingertips together. 'I do believe that you rescued me.'

'*Everybody* did. But I pulled hard on the rope. So did Boy. He's skinny as a match, but he eats porridge so he's strong. He's coming around to see us tomorrow.'

'It is a pity you did not get your dance after all.'

'When your ankle's better maybe *you* can show me how to dance. I don't reckon *you'd* stomp on my feet.'

'Perhaps.'

Audrey guessed that this 'perhaps' was really a 'yes'.

'It would be good to learn how to dance now that my project is finished,' added Audrey. 'At first it was hard to find things on your good side. But then it got easier. You've got one, all right.'

'That is a great comfort to me.' Mrs Paterson looked over at Douglas. 'If your little brother is to be believed, he has kissed a snail.'

'Yes, he has.'

'Have you ever touched one?'

'Yes, it pulls in its head and hides in its shell.'

'Precisely.' Mrs Paterson clasped her hands together. 'I have been like a snail, hiding in my shell.'

'You came out of your shell, didn't you?'

'I suppose I did,' said Mrs Paterson.

'There are lots of funny people here. But you look after each other.'

'I have friends after all.'

'I've got some new friends here too. And my family's getting bigger.' Audrey counted on her fingers. 'Mum, Dad, Price, Douglas, Pearl, Esther, Sassafras, Buttons, an Expecting and Stumpy.'

Mrs Paterson's eyebrow went up again at the mention of Stumpy. Luckily, she didn't know he was hiding in the bedroom because it was cold outside.

'Now I'm adoptinating *you*,' added Audrey. 'And Lionel and Mr Paterson. People can still be in your family, even when they only live inside your head.'

Mrs Paterson's face moved as though she wanted to say something, but no words came out.

'So, d'ya reckon I'll go home a lady?' asked Audrey.

'You were a lady when you arrived,' said Mrs Paterson. 'I simply did not recognise it. A lady is kind and thinks of others. You do that very well.'

She adjusted the rug over her knees. 'When your hands are better we will resume our knitting lessons. I will knit socks for Mr Jenkins. After tonight, he will need a new pair.'

'Can I do red, like your thing with the arms? I like red.'

'That *thing* will be a cardigan,' said Mrs Paterson. 'You may start with a scarf, and we will see how you go.'

'Should we shake hands on it, like Dad does?'

'I think we trust each other, don't you?'

Audrey nodded. 'I reckon it's another one of those miroolcools.'

Interesting Words

Billy: tin container used to boil
                        water when camping
                        outdoors

Blowfly: a fly which deposits eggs or
                        legless larvae (maggots) in
                        carcasses, meat, sores or
                        wounds

Chook: domestic chicken

Cockatoo: a crested parrot

'Cocky's corsets':   Something good

'Come a cropper':   fall

Cooee: a call used to attract
                        attention in the bush. It
                        rises in pitch on the last
                        syllable—ee.

Dingo: Australian wild dog, often
                        brownish-yellow with
                        pointy ears. It doesn't bark,
                        but howls. Dingoes are
                        known for attacking farm
                        animals, such as sheep.

Dogger:	someone who catches dingoes for payment
Dray:	a cart with no sides, used for heavy loads
Drover:	Someone who drives cattle to a market, often over a long distance
Dunny:	outside toilet
Fair dinkum:	true
Goanna:	a large Australian monitor lizard
Gully:	a small valley, usually cut by water
Hander:	to be hit on the hand at school as a punishment
Hessian:	coarse, rough cloth made from jute, used for sacks or carpet backing
'Knock me bandy':	to be surprised
Koala:	a furry, grey, Australian marsupial with big ears, that lives in gum trees
Lanoline:	fat from sheep's wool

Meat safe:	a cabinet which keeps food cool. When a breeze blows through wet fabric, such as hessian, it keeps the temperature low inside the cabinet.
Possum:	Australian marsupial that lives in trees and is most active at night
Quandong:	Australian native fruit that grows on trees
Saltbush:	hardy, low-growing drought-resistant plant found in the Australian bush
Squeezebox:	accordion
Swaggie (or swagman):	a bush traveller who carries a swag (a bundle of belongings) on his or her back, often earning money from odd jobs or gifts
Tank stand:	a framework to support a rainwater tank
The big spit:	vomit
Tucker:	food

Look out for other titles in the **Audrey** series . . .

Audrey of the Outback

Meet Audrey Barlow—a girl with a lot on her mind. Her dad has gone away to work, her brother Price thinks he's too old for games, and little Dougie likes pretending to be a bird. But at least she's not alone. Audrey has a friend that is like no other, one who leads her to the hardest decision she has ever made.

Audrey's Big Secret

Audrey Barlow has a secret. What will she do about it? She is torn between keeping a promise and telling the truth. Should she keep the secret or tell her family?

Choices are never easy. Especially when someone could be hurt.